BB pressed the handlebars. Nearer and nearer they headed for the gap in the wall. Ben looked over BB's shoulder at the approaching gap, with just empty space beyond.

'We're getting a bit close,' he said, worried.

'Don't worry,' said BB. 'It'll be like it was before. It'll work at the last minute.'

Nervously, Ben turned to see where the pursuing soldiers were, and it was then he noticed the leads trailing uselessly from the black box on the pillion of the bike. The Time Unit wasn't connected! They were heading off the edge of the castle wall into empty space!

The following books by the same author also available in Red Fox (incorporating Beaver Books)

By Jim and Duncan Eldridge

Bad Boyes
Bad Boyes and the Gangsters
Bogeys, Boils and Belly Buttons
How to Handle Grown Ups
More Ways to Handle Grown Ups
What Grown Ups Say and What They Really Mean
Peregrine Peabody's Completely Misleading Guide to Sport
Peregrine Peabody's Completely Misleading History of the World
Complete How to Handle Grown Ups (3-in-1)

By Jim Eldridge

Completely Misleading Guide to School
The Holidays Survival Guide
The Wobbly Jelly Joke Book
Uncle Jack and Operation Green
Potts
Uncle Jack and the Loch Noch Monster

Time Riders
by Jim Eldridge

Illustrated by
Mark Robertson

RED FOX

A Red Fox Book
Published by Random Century Children's Books
20 Vauxhall Bridge Road, London SW1V 2SA

A division of the Random Century Group
London Melbourne Sydney Auckland
Johannesburg and agencies throughout the world

First published by Red Fox 1991

Set in Times
Typeset by JH Graphics Ltd, Reading

Printed and bound in Great Britain by
Cox & Wyman Ltd, Reading, Berkshire

ISBN 0 09 993940 1

Time Riders

Chapter One

It wasn't so much that time travel was difficult, thought Dr BB Miller; the real problem lay in persuading the rest of the scientific establishment that it was even possible, and that it didn't rank alongside such things as Believing That the Earth Was Flat, and That Babies Are Brought By The Stork (although, BB reflected, with the recent advances in Genetic Engineering anything was possible as far as producing babies was concerned).

She looked around her laboratory and sighed. Here she was, twenty-nine years old with two science degrees, an M.Sc in molecular physics, and a PhD in quantum sub-atomic structures, and yet her laboratory did not even begin to compare in looks or equipment with the rest of the science building here at the university. It was different for all the other scientists on the upper floors who were working on things like weapons research or animal experiments (usually with some grand-sounding name to make it seem different from what it actually was: titles like Semi-Automatic Dissimilation Process Research — which meant 'blowing things up'). They all had wonderful laboratories that looked like something out of a space station. Here she was, in the basement of the building, with equipment that looked as if she'd constructed most of it herself.

In fact, she *had* constructed most of it herself, mainly because for the kind of research in which she was involved there was no existing equipment.

She sat down on the seat of her Yamaha 750 motorcycle and looked at her time machine. As her hand stroked the seat of her precious motorcycle, she reflected that here was another example of the shabby way she was treated at this place. All the professors and doctors of this and that, even some of the junior technicians, had their own parking space allocated in the science building car park. Why? Because they were working on what was considered orthodox science. Yet she was forced to keep her precious bike here in her laboratory when she was at work because there was no secure parking space for it.

Twice when she had left it out in the general car park someone had tampered with it, trying to steal it. Good grief! she fumed to herself, even the man who cleans the basement corridor has a proper secure parking place for his bicycle!

Still, she thought ruefully, that was the price you had to pay if you were interested in breaking new barriers in science. The establishment had always sneered at genuine innovators in scientific research: Galileo, Newton, Einstein. The day would come when they would be smiling at her instead of sneering, praising her instead of laughing at her behind her back.

She got off the bike and went over to her time machine. Next to the time machine was a small clutter of objects, each damaged in some way: a small pewter goblet with a dent in it; a piece of cracked flint; a watch with a damaged face; a scorched photograph. Each of these had one thing in common: they had all been sent back in time by BB, and then returned to the present and the dust on them carbon-dated to establish their authenticity as having travelled in time. The first few times had been failures, the dust had burnt up in the process of

8

travelling in time so BB had been unable to verify to which period they had been sent. But these last two times . . .

Her thoughts were interrupted by the door of her laboratory opening, and Professor Crow, head of the Science Faculty at the university, entering.

Professor Crow was an imposing figure, tall with a shock of white hair almost like a lion's mane. Always smartly and impeccably dressed, he was in his early sixties, and vain to the point where he treated all the other workers (and that included even the senior scientists) in the science building as if he were a Lord of the Manor and they were the peasants who looked up to him. Or, if they didn't, then as if they should. Crow's one driving ambition in life was to achieve a Nobel prize. Frankly, he didn't care in what, he would have even settled for a Nobel Prize in Tiddlywinks, but he wanted *his* name on that list of Nobel Prizewinners. He had wanted this when he was in his early twenties, but it had never happened. Now he was in his sixties, it seemed an even more remote possibility. His only chance, he realized, lay in one of the scientists under his command coming up with some major scientific discovery, with Crow taking most of the credit.

The one person that would *not* be, he reflected as he looked around BB's laboratory, was Dr BB Miller. He did his best to force a smile and hide his well-known dislike of what he considered this 'fraud' that Dr Miller was perpetuating. Time travel indeed! Straight out of comics and television!

BB was surprised to see the head of the Science Faculty actually enter her laboratory. She was surprised that such an important person as Crow should even know where it was, tucked away here in the basement.

'Professor Crow,' she said. 'I don't often see you in the lower reaches of the science block.'

Crow smiled a smooth politician's smile.

'Well, time travel is not exactly a 'mainstream' science, is it?' he said.

'Only at the moment,' countered BB. 'I'm glad you're here because I've been wanting to explain to you my theory, but whenever I try to get hold of you, you're usually busy.'

'Yes, I'm afraid I often am,' said Crow, though he didn't sound sorry. In truth, the last thing he wanted was to have to listen to this young woman expounding her crackpot theories of how to travel in time.

BB, however, wasn't going to let this opportunity slip. She'd been longing to explain her theory to someone.

'The whole thing is based on the Moebius effect, which pushes objects inside out, like when you take a rubber glove off,' explained BB. 'This does the same thing with time.'

Crow groaned, inwardly.

'Perhaps some other time, Dr Miller. . . ,' he began. 'What I have to see you about. . . .'

But BB was not going to let this chance go without letting Crow have the works. She had already moved over to her time machine, a large empty cube made of chrome rods, with digital displays. Beneath this chrome cube, and attached to it by various wires, was a small black box about the size of an ordinary video recorder.

BB pointed to the black box.

'This is the energy amplifier. It generates an energy field inside the framework of the actual time machine, this chrome cube here. The energy field affects any

10

object, organic or inorganic, which is in contact with the energy amplifier, breaking that object down into its constituent atoms.

'Once the object has been broken down, the atoms are sucked by vacuum magnetics into the energy amplifier through an absorber grille. As soon as the atoms are inside the energy amplifier, the time machine "cage" receives a surge of power from an accelerator inside the box, which pushes it through a quantum leap for the Moebius effect. This Moebius effect literally turns the cage inside out: as I said, like a rubber glove being turned inside out.

'This inside out rolling movement caused by the Moebius effect continues and the cube is then turned inside out again from its "inside out" state, so that it returns to its normal appearance. An energy field is then automatically transmitted from the energy amplifier. Once this energy field has been established the atoms held inside the energy amplifier transfer by vacuum de-magnetism into the energy field and reassemble into their original shape.

'The combination of the quantum leap with the Moebius effect means that the energy amplifier has made a space-time continuum jump, and that object now occupies the same *space* as previously, but in a different *time*.

'As the energy amplifier goes through the quantum leap its own particles sub-divide like amoeba and so two identical energy fields exist: one in the laboratory, and one with the object in the new "time". This is necessary in order to ensure that I can recall the object from its journey into time.

'Over here. . . .'

And BB was already on her way towards a small

11

side room off her laboratory, effectively her control room for her time machine.

Crow, still suffering from shock after this verbal battering, decided he had had enough.

'Over here on this VDU unit appear the images of the particular time through which the energy field is passing . . .' BB was just saying, when:

'Dr Miller. . . !' snapped Crow imperiously, following it up with a surprising tone of disgust as he said 'Urghhhh!'

BB stopped talking about her portable VDU and looked round at Crow. She saw that, as he had moved forward, he had unfortunately stepped into a tray of waste sump oil in whch she was soaking some nuts belonging to her motorcycle.

'Mind out!' said BB, alarmed. It was so easy for nuts to disappear, and you could never get the right size straight away. She rushed over to the tray as Crow removed his now oily shoe from it and poked around in the oil. Yes, they were still there. She stood up and gave Crow a smile of relief. 'I've got four nuts soaking in that tray. Luckily they're still there, so everything's all right.'

Crow stared at her, almost too shocked to speak.

'All right?' He pointed at his oily shoe with a finger that twitched with indignation. 'This shoe came from Italy!'

'Really?' said BB, trying to lighten the situation. 'Where did the other one come from?'

One look at the angry expression on Crow's face told her that this had not been a wise remark to make.

'Sorry,' BB apologized humbly. 'Just trying to make you feel better about it. Italian, eh?' She decided to try to recover the conversation with some light chat on the Italian theme. After all, Professor Crow was *the* most important person in the science block. 'There's a great Italian restaurant just opened in the town. Have you seen it? The Trattoria del Desmond. The owner isn't exactly Italian, actually he's Irish, but he likes Italian cars . . .'

'Dr Miller,' said Crow curtly.

BB stopped and looked at Crow. She could tell, from the tone of his voice and the expression on his face, that any mood that he might have felt in for a light chat had vanished.

'I did not come here to talk about Italian food or Italian cars.'

'Oh?' said BB.

Crow pointed at her motorcycle.

'I came here to talk about that.' ·

BB felt both relieved and proud. If there was one thing she liked talking about, apart from her research into time travel, it was her motorbike, the pride of her life.

'Isn't it wonderful!' she exclaimed. 'D'you know where it should be?'

'Yes,' said Crow. 'In a garage.'

BB shook her head, a look of pride in her eyes as she gazed in adoration upon her precious Yamaha.

'In an Art Gallery. If Van Gogh had made motor-bikes, this is the sort he would have made.'

Crow did not seem impressed.

'This morning I had a report from Security that on four separate occasions recently, despite being ordered not to, you have brought that thing into the building instead of leaving it in the car park where it belongs.'

'Thing?!' choked BB, shocked.

'I am here, Dr Miller, to ask why you are keeping that vehicle in what is supposed to be a science laboratory. And I emphasize "supposed".'

'Because. . . ,' began BB, about to describe the attempts to tamper and steal her precious bike, but Crow was now in full flood as the pent-up feelings he had long held about BB Miller and her research came out.

'But while I am here I would like to make a more general point,' he continued.

'Shoot,' said BB.

'If I had a gun I would, and the first thing I would shoot would be that thing.'

And Crow pointed his indignant twitching finger at BB's time machine.

BB was even further shocked. First to insult her Yamaha, and now to do the same thing to her time machine! This was outrageous!

'My time machine?! Why?'

'Because it is a fraud!'

'A fraud?' BB bristled as only an insulted scientist can. 'How dare you! The Ethereal Research Foundation have enough belief in my research to give me funding . . .'

'Just because you have persuaded a bunch of half-dead morons to give you a research grant. . . !' thundered Crow.

'They are not half-dead!' retorted BB indignantly. On a note of reluctant qualification, because she was an honest woman, she added: 'All right, one or two of them may be made up of spare parts, but we can't all be perfect.'

'None of them would know a science experiment from the holes in their nostrils!' snapped Crow. 'That money should be spent on proper scientific research!'

'Like yours?' demanded BB. Now they were getting to the root of the matter. Crow was jealous of her funding.

'Yes!' said Crow.

'Ha!' BB snapped back with great scorn.

'Don't you "Ha!" me. . . !' growled Crow, stepping forward aggressively towards BB, and then stopping with another disgusted 'Urghhh!'

BB and Crow looked down as Crow took his other foot out of the tray of waste oil.

'Now they match,' said BB, trying to be helpful.

'This fraud. . . !' persisted Crow.

BB stepped past him, picked up a crash helmet and placed it in the centre of the chrome cube time machine.

'Do you see this?' she demanded.

'Yes, and at last I know what this thing is: a wardrobe.'

BB ignored the jibe.

'A hundred and sixty years ago on this very spot was a courthouse,' she said. 'Today I am sending that crash helmet back in time to that courthouse.'

'You think they're in desperate need of a crash helmet, do you?'

'When it returns I will carbon date the dust . . .'

'Oh really!' scoffed Crow. 'What sort of idiot do you think I am?'

'The sort who treads in oil. Twice.'

Crow stiffened. How dare she! He would show this insolent young woman that *he* was in charge of this science building, and everyone in it.

'Listen, Miller, I will say this just once. I am going to get you out of this science block and return this lab to the use for which it was intended: proper scientific research. I will not have you wasting much-needed funds on this . . . this . . . this charlatanism!'

And with that Crow stormed over to the door and left, slamming the door behind him.

BB glared at the door, fuming with rage at Crow's dismissive treatment of all her hard work.

'You are an idiot with the imagination of a lemon!' she shouted at the door, which opened again almost immediately and Crow glared in at her.

'What?' asked Crow.

BB forced a smile.

'Have a nice day,' she said.

Crow scowled and slammed the door again.

BB walked through to her control room, fuming with indignation.

'Fraud, indeed!'

She went to the control panel and began to press buttons and adjust dials, setting digital displays that lit up the black box at the base of the time machine.

'I'll show that moron Crow,' she said. 'When that crash helmet comes back, I'll make him eat it.'

And she set the digital display for the Target Date at 1832, made a last adjustment to the energy field amplifier control, and pressed the button marked: 'ACTIVATE'.

Chapter Two

Ben Hardy — or Benjamin, as was his full and given name — was thirteen years old and had been living on the streets of London since he was orphaned in 1829 at the age of ten. By the age of eleven he was a proficient shoplifter, by the age of twelve he was a nimble-fingered pickpocket. Not that he had wanted to be a criminal, it was just that as a poor orphan he had been presented with three simple choices: the workhouse, starvation, or petty crime.

Not that he considered pickpocketing a crime. After all, he only took what he needed to support himself. To Ben, dipping his hand in now and then for food or a little money was far less of a crime than what went on in the workhouse. He had spent time in the workhouse with his mother the year before she died, and it had been the treatment she had received in there that had killed her. Now *that* had been a crime.

Unfortunately, society in general did not share Ben's view, which was why he now found himself in court at the age of thirteen, peering over the top of the dock at a large red-faced man wearing a dirty white wig. This was the infamous 'Hanging' Judge Johnson.

A rabble of onlookers packed the court. For them this was another great day's entertainment. Already there had been one man sentenced to transportation because he was behind with a debt, and a woman sentenced to hang because she had caused trouble at the workhouse. 'Subversion and Insurrection', Judge Johnson had called it, though everyone knew all she had done was bitten the nose of the Beadle, a notoriously vicious man who most people believed deserved to have all of him bitten, and by dogs rather than by people. However, now the entertainment was taking the form of this small thin waif in the dock, held in place there by two tall and muscular policemen.

Judge Johnson looked down at his notes, which (as anyone who examined them closely would have seen) were actually doodles and drawings.

'Benjamin Hardy,' he intoned, 'you have been found guilty of stealing a loaf of bread. . . .'

'It was only one slice, your honour, and I was hungry. . . ,' said Ben in his defence.

Judge Johnson smiled, and the audience in the court rubbed their hands gleefully. This was the smile they liked. It always meant that the Judge had something particularly nasty up his sleeve. Ben, however, saw the smile and forced one back. Maybe he was going to get off after all?

'Well, you'll never be hungry again,' said the Judge.

Ben's smile broadened.

'Cor, fanks, yer honour!' he said.

His smile vanished as he heard the Judge's next words.

'I sentence you to be hanged by the neck until you are completely and utterly dead.'

The crowd in the court applauded. Brilliant! Ben stared at the Judge, shocked.

'Take him out and hang him,' ordered the Judge.

'Come on, you,' growled one of the two policemen, and touched Ben on the shoulder.

If you think you're going to hang me, you're mistaken! thought Ben, and he slammed one of his feet down hard on the policeman's instep.

'Aarghh!!' yelled the policeman.

It was a matter of seconds for Ben to jump up on the edge of the dock and leap for the public gallery, heading for the door out of the court and the street beyond and freedom. The crowd in the court, however, were in no mood to let their fun disappear like that.

'Grab the boy!' yelled Judge Johnson, and he lurched up from his huge chair and searched for something to throw at Ben.

Ben, meanwhile, had found his exits barred as all the doors of the court were shut and locked. Frantically, he ran around the court, searching for a window, an opening of any sort that would lead him out of this place. As he ran, he punched and kicked, fending off police and members of the public alike as they tried to stop him.

Suddenly two strong hands grabbed him and he found himself staring into the evil grinning face of Judge Johnson. The stench of the man's hideous breath made Ben recoil.

'Got you!' said the Judge, laughing.

Then, suddenly, blue flashes began to dart all over Ben's body, electric sparks ran all over his clothes and skin. The Judge drew back from the boy in horror. Ben stared down at himself. What was happening? Was it spontaneous combustion? Was he going to explode? The crowd looked at this sudden apparition in horror, some of them closing their eyes, others gaping at Ben in eerie fascination.

There was a blinding white flash from where the boy stood and everyone in the court recoiled, shielding their eyes. When they opened them a second later and looked, where Ben had stood was . . . nothing.

* * *

'Back you come, crash helmet!'

And BB pressed the 'RECALL' button on the control panel in front of her. She looked through the window at the time machine in the actual laboratory. There seemed to be a shape forming, shimmering in the centre of the chrome cube.

'Come on!' said BB, shivering slightly with excitement. This would be the largest object yet she had sent back through time. This would be the one that would certainly give her the proof she needed!

She pressed the 'RECALL' button again, and there was a blinding flash from the centre of the cube as her time machine blew up in front of her eyes, sending the broken chrome rods spinning across the laboratory to crash against the window, flame-lit smoke pouring out from the machine, filling the laboratory, then sudden darkness as all the power was cut off.

Chapter Three

Professor Crow and his assistant, Hepworth, were about to dissect a rat in Crow's laboratory when the power failure occurred.

There were times when Crow had misgivings about Hepworth. The man was good at his job, it was true, but he was almost *too* good. Sometimes Crow felt that Hepworth took a particular pleasure in cutting things up, especially living things, and that feeling disturbed him.

Crow was quite right. Hepworth did like cutting things up. He liked nothing better than opening up a creature and removing various organs which he could then 'play with'. Most of all he liked examining brains, but very few ever really came his way. By the time he got one the subject that had used it was dead. What Hepworth had always wanted was a living brain that he could keep and examine in detail. Maybe he could even keep it in a jar at his home and train it to talk to him.

Now he and Crow were poised over a rat which was held down to a table by electronic grabs. In his hand Hepworth held a scalpel, and he was just about to make his first incision, when everything went dark.

'What. . . ?' began Crow.

Then the lights went on again, and when Hepworth looked the electronic grabs were open and the rat had escaped.

Almost immediately a white-coated technician rushed into the lab.

'What on earth happened?' demanded Crow. 'We were in the middle of an important experiment!'

'There was a sudden power failure,' said the technician. 'However the standby generator's cut in so we've got power. All except the basement, where the fault happened. . . .'

Crow's nostrils dilated in anger and for a moment both Hepworth and the technician actually thought he was going to breathe out fire.

'Miller!' he raged, and he strode for the door. 'Hepworth! Follow me!'

* * *

In BB's laboratory, BB had managed to lay her hands on a torch and was now adjusting her eyes to seeing through the smoke-filled gloom with the aid of the torch's beam.

She stumbled into the main laboratory, trying to wave away the clouds of acrid smoke, using one arm as a fan. Her time machine was a mess, the chrome rods broken and twisted, electrical wires hanging melted. And there, sitting in the middle of the wreckage, and wearing her crash helmet, was a small boy in ragged clothes.

BB bristled! How dare he! This boy had obviously crept in while her back was turned and had somehow or other interfered with the mechanics of the time machine, causing it to blow up! It was lucky he hadn't been killed, though when she got her hands on him that situation might well change.

BB stormed towards the boy, furious. She would show him!

'Who are you, and what are you doing in my machine?!' she yelled at him.

The boy took off the crash helmet and stared at her, bewildered, and then his face broke into a broad grin.

'A jailbreak!' he grinned. 'Brilliant!'

A jailbreak? thought BB, baffled. Then her nose twitched. Urgh! This boy stank!

She didn't have time to say any more, because suddenly the door to her laboratory was wrenched open and Professor Crow stormed in. Behind him came the small and malevolent figure of Hepworth, taking great pleasure in the catastrophe.

'So!' raged Crow.

Uh-oh, thought BB. Now I *am* in trouble. Aloud she said apologetically: 'Professor Crow . . .'

'Do you realize you just caused a power cut to the whole science building?' stormed Crow.

'Ten million pounds worth of ruined experiments!' added Hepworth gleefully. 'They'll kill you!'

'I don't know what happened. . . ,' BB tried again, but Crow's attention was suddenly taken by the small boy sliding towards the door of the laboratory.

'Oh no you don't!' snarled Crow, and he grabbed Ben by the collar. 'Who is this object?' he demanded of BB.

BB shook her head helplessly.

'I don't know . . .'

Crow glared at Ben.

'Who are you?' he shouted.

Ben gulped and tried a smile.

'Ben Hardy, yer honour. Just passing through . . .'

Suddenly Crow realized what BB was trying to stage, and he turned to her, a sneer on his face.

26

'Oh, a very good try, Dr Miller,' he said sarcastically.

'Look. . . ,' began BB helplessly, totally out of her depth, but Crow had now thrust Ben towards Hepworth.

'A genuine Victorian street urchin, Hepworth. How original.'

Hepworth grabbed hold of Ben and began to poke the boy's face with his bony fingers, a smile on his lips.

'I wonder what else she has for us, Professor?' he cackled. 'Lord Nelson? A boatload of marauding Vikings?'

Again BB tried to put her defence: 'Professor Crow. . . ' she began.

Crow stopped her with an imperious wave of his hand.

'Enough,' he said. 'I'll see you in my office at four o'clock and we can finalize the closure of this so-called "research unit", and its return to proper science. Until then the electricity supply to this laboratory will not be restored. Come, Hepworth.'

And with that Crow headed for the basement corridor. Hepworth continued holding on to Ben for a moment longer, a thoughtful frown on his face, before he released the boy and followed Crow. As he went out of the laboratory he cast one last thoughtful look back at Ben, before shutting the door behind him.

When the two men had gone, Ben let out a deep sigh of relief.

'Coo! They ain't too happy, are they? Anyway, if you'll point me to the way out, I'll be on my way.'

'Oh no you don't!' said the angry BB, grabbing him so that he couldn't run off. If this boy thought he was just going to walk out like this after the way he had

27

ruined not only her experiment but possibly her whole career, then he had another think coming! 'Who are you. . . ?'

'I told you: Ben Hardy.'

'And how did you get in here?'

'I dunno,' admitted Ben, still a bit baffled by recent events. 'I was in this court . . .'

BB's mouth dropped open as the implication of what Ben had just said hit her. It couldn't be. . . !

'Quick!' she said. 'What's the date?'

Ben looked at her, worried by her obvious intensity.

'Monday,' he said, and hoped it was the right answer. She looked the sort of woman who'd bash him if she wanted it to be Tuesday.

'No, you idiot. The year!' yelled BB.

'1832, of course,' said Ben. 'Why?'

'Oh Lord!' said BB, stunned. 'Oh Lord! I did it! I have sent a person through time!'

Ben looked at her, baffled. Sent someone through time?

'Who?' he asked.

'You! I have made history!'

Ben stared at her, still not sure what this strange woman was going on about.

The lack of light in the lab, apart from the beam from the torch, suddenly irritated BB.

'Let's get some light on the subject,' she said, and she strode over to her Yamaha, started it up and switched on the headlight.

The shock of this machine suddenly being switched on with a low but terrifying roar, and the dazzling glare from the headlight, made Ben cower back. What was this? Where was he? What was this strange machine?

BB, still hanging on to Ben, paced around the lab, thinking furiously.

'If I could only get the time machine working again before I see Crow, he'd *have* to believe me,' she said aloud, and then she groaned in frustration: 'But I've got no power!'

Ben pointed towards the motorbike, still baffled at what was happening.

'How did you do that?' he asked.

BB looked at the bike and was about to explain what a motorcycle was, when suddenly an illumination hit her. The motorbike! Of course! Fix HT leads to the engine and that would give her the power she needed!

She released Ben and dusted him off.

'Right, we've got till four o'clock,' she said determinedly. 'Let's get to work! And while we're doing it, I'll explain a few things to you . . .'

Chapter Four

Crow and Hepworth were almost back at Crow's laboratory when Hepworth put his thoughts into spoken words.

'There's one thing that puzzles me, Professor,' he said.

'Only one?' chuckled Crow, amused at his joke.

'I'm talking about Miller and her time machine.'

'Her "so-called" time machine,' snapped Crow.

'Of course,' grovelled Hepworth. 'But what I wondered was: how did she smuggle the child into the building, considering how tight security is.'

Crow stopped as the implication behind Hepworth's words struck him.

'Not that there's anything in this time-travelling business, of course,' added Hepworth quickly.

'Of course there isn't!' scoffed Crow.

'It's just that, if there *were* rumours about this, it would be just the sort of ridiculous thing that undeserving people like her get Nobel Prizes for.'

At the magic words 'Nobel Prize', Crow's eyes lit up momentarily. Then his face settled into a thoughtful frown and he continued on into his laboratory, Hepworth trailing after him.

* * *

BB was hard at work disconnecting pieces of equipment from her control panel and re-connecting them to the black box energy amplifier, while connecting the whole lot to the engine of the Yamaha. Luckily for her the black box energy amplifier, the core of her whole time machine, had been undamaged in the explosion, just scorched slightly.

She looked up to see Ben wandering around in what she called her 'domestic room', a small kitchenette complete with cooker, telephone, television. When she was working late it meant that she was at least able to fix herself something to eat. The boy was picking up things and sniffing at them, getting used to all this unfamiliar stuff. He seemed to have taken the news of what had happened to him quite calmly, saying he was glad to get out of the time he had been living in.

She fixed the HT leads back in place, then started the bike up and watched the dials record the power input. Not enough revs. She would need actually to run the bike to get enough power to make the time machine work.

Inside the domestic room Ben was fascinated by all the strange objects he was encountering.

He picked up something that looked like a dog's bone, only it had buttons with numbers on it. He pressed some of the buttons, and suddenly a woman's voice spoke to him out of one end of the bone: 'Hello?'

Alarmed, Ben dropped the bone back on the table and sat down heavily on a chair, on the remote control for the television.

Instantly the small portable television came on and a man looked out at Ben and began to talk to him about world problems.

Ben gulped, jumped up, and pointed at the television.

'There's a man's head in that box!' he yelled.

BB came in, picked up the remote control, and switched the television off.

'I told you to leave things alone,' she reprimanded him. Then she returned to thinking about the problems of temporarily rebuilding the time machine: 'If I set the energy field to the physical boundaries of the energy amplifier . . .'

'Is this going to take long?' grumbled Ben. 'I'm hungry.'

BB shook her head, amazed at the lack of interest this child seemed to have in the miracles of science.

'You don't seem to understand what's happened here,' she pointed out. 'You have travelled in time! All we have to do is prove it! How long have I got before Crow expects me?'

And she looked at her wrist, only to find that the watch that she always wore had gone. For a moment she was puzzled and she stood looking around the laboratory, saying:

'Where's my watch?'

'What watch?' said Ben, with an uncomfortable innocence.

'You've got it!' BB suddenly realized, and she grabbed the startled Ben and thrust her hand into one of his coat pockets.

'Get off!' protested Ben, struggling, but he began to quieten down as BB produced various items of hers that Ben had obviously picked up in his search of her domestic room.

From his other pocket BB took out her watch. She released him with a look of scorn and put her watch back on.

'How did that get there?' said Ben, trying to look surprised.

'You are a despicable little thief!' snapped BB.

'I'm not little!' protested Ben.

BB's nose wrinkled. She had been so busy with her work that she had forgotten the overpowering odour from the boy that had first struck her about him.

'You also smell,' she said. 'Come on.'

And she took hold of Ben's collar and began to march him towards the door of the laboratory.

'Where we going?' asked Ben, worried by this sudden urgency of movement.

'If I'm going to show you off. . . ,' said BB.

'Show me off?' said Ben indignantly.

'You're my evidence,' BB reminded him. 'And at the moment you're smelly evidence, so you're going to be cleaned up first. You're going for a bath.'

'A bath?!' Ben was obviously outraged at the suggestion.

'Right,' said BB.

And with that she marched him out of the laboratory and headed for the boiler room, where there was a bath and a washing machine.

* * *

The cleaning of Ben was not one of the greatest experiences that either BB or Ben had ever known. Ben had been suspicious of the washing machine, which he considered was 'grinding my clothes up.'

The actual bath was an event that he resisted strongly, claiming that 'baths caused germs', but eventually BB managed to get him into the tub and scrubbed clean, even though she did end up almost as wet as Ben in the process.

However, eventually they were able to head back to

the laboratory with Ben looking almost clean, and certainly smelling sweeter than he had in all his thirteen years.

When they walked back in a surprise awaited them in the two persons of Professor Crow and Hepworth.

BB stopped, apprehensively. Crow was early. It obviously meant bad news. Maybe they were going to kick her out of the science building immediately, before she'd had a chance to reproduce her successful time-travelling experiment.

Crow smiled.

'I see you have returned with the specimen, Dr Miller,' he said approvingly.

BB didn't pick him up on his use of the word 'specimen'. She forced a smile and hoped she could win him round by sweetness, if not by logic.

'Look, Professor Crow,' she said appealingly, 'I know it's hard for you to believe but this boy really has come from the past.'

'Yes, I believe he may well have,' said Crow.

BB looked first at Crow and then at Hepworth. Neither of them looked as if they were joking, although Hepworth seemed to be smothering a smile of pleasure.

'You do?' she asked suspiciously.

'The problem, of course, is in verifying our research,' said Crow.

'That's no problem. . . !' began BB delightedly, and then she stopped. '*Our* research. . . ?'

'I am head of this faculty, so any research carried out in this building. . . ,' Crow reminded her airily.

BB stared at him, furious.

'An hour ago you were saying you didn't believe in it.'

'My little joke,' smiled Crow.

'A joke?' said BB. 'This work . . .'

'This work could become mine exclusively, Dr Miller,' Crow pointed out to her, his voice now steely, and BB fell silent and just fumed inwardly as Crow continued: 'As I was saying, we need to prove if this child actually has come from the past. So Hepworth and I would like to examine him. Isn't that right. Hepworth?'

BB looked at the pair suspiciously.

'Examine him?'

'The usual tests,' purred Hepworth. 'Sonar scanners. Carbon dating. The Mendeleyev tests using the periodic table.'

The matter-of-fact way he said it sent shivers running down BB's spine. She stared at him aghast.

'The Mendeleyev test?!'

Ben, now looking very worried, started to back towards the door, but Crow's hand reached out and took hold of him firmly.

'Don't worry,' he smiled down at the boy. 'You won't feel a thing.'

BB was still shocked at the thought of Hepworth and Crow using the Mendeleyev test on Ben.

'But that means . . . you're going to *irradiate* him?!'

Ben grew even more worried. He didn't know what it meant to have this 'irradiate' business done to you, but it didn't sound very good for his health.

'He's a child! A living human being!' BB beseeched them.

'I am!' nodded Ben energetically.

'If he's come from the past he's an object for legitimate scientific research,' pointed out Crow. 'As a scientist you must know that.'

'Also, if he's here as a result of your experiment,

36

then he doesn't officially exist, does he?' added Hepworth, enjoying himself immensely.

With that Hepworth took one of Ben's arms and with Crow holding Ben's other arm they steered the boy out of BB's lab.

BB followed them, feeling impotent in the face of Crow's power, but still appalled at the treatment they had in store for Ben.

'You don't fool me with your nice words and your smile, Professor Crow! I know what goes on in your lab! You're a disgrace to science!' she bellowed after them.

Crow and Hepworth smiled down at Ben and continued on their way.

'Take no notice of her,' said Crow. 'She's just jealous.'

Chapter Five

As Ben was half-walked, half-dragged along the basement corridor by Crow and Hepworth, his eyes darted about him constantly, looking for a way of escape. But this building was unlike anything he'd ever seen before. Where were the windows? It was like one of the underground passages at the workhouse, but the workhouse had never looked like this, all shiny and clean with all these people walking around in white coats.

The two men stopped Ben outside a door made of a silver sort of metal. One of the men pushed a button on the wall and the metal door slid open and Ben saw that in front of him was a large box made of metal, big enough for six people to stand in. Was this it? Was this the box where they were going to do this irradiate thing to him? He gulped and tensed, ready to run, but Crow and Hepworth pushed him into the box and came in with him. Hepworth pressed a button near the door, and the metal door slid shut again.

Suddenly Ben felt that he was being pushed down, although no-one was touching him. Then he realized what was happening! The box was moving upwards!

He was about to throw himself down on to the floor before something terrible happened, when the metal door slid open again.

Ben looked around goggle-eyed as Crow and

Hepworth hauled him out of the metal box. The corridor had changed. Now there were windows! They were on a different floor altogether! This metal box must be like stairs, except that you didn't have to walk up.

As the trio walked along, Ben reflected that if that was all this irradiate business was about, it didn't hurt very much.

'Carbon dating the bone marrow and skin would be useful as well . . . ' said Hepworth to Crow, over Ben's head.

Crow hissed 'Quiet, you fool!', and gave Ben one of his smiles that certainly didn't fool Ben.

As they walked on down a corridor, now filled with cages on either side that contained dogs and cats and mice and rats, Ben thought over Hepworth's words. Carbon dating bone marrow and skin? Well whatever this 'carbon dating' was they couldn't do that to his skin because he was still wearing it. Unless . . .

As the horrific thought hit him, Ben stopped dead in his tracks. They were going to cut him up!

'Come on,' said Crow tersely, and tugged at Ben's arm.

Oh no! thought Ben. There was no way they were going to cut him in pieces to find out what he was made of! He kicked out twice sharply, connecting with both Crow's and Hepworth's shins in rapid succession, and the two men let go of Ben's arms and began to hop around the corridor, clutching their injured legs.

'Get him!' screamed Crow as Ben turned and made a run for it along the corridor. 'Stop that boy!'

No-one's stopping me, thought Ben with grim determination, and he put his head down as he ran to charge anyone out of the way who tried to stop him. It was with his head down that he ran smack! full-tilt into a trolley full of scientific equipment just as it was wheeled round the corner, his head hitting the solid metal front of the trolley with a resounding crash.

He hung in front of the trolley for a second as the technician pushing it stared at the boy in horror, then crashed to the floor, out cold.

* * *

When Ben came round the first thing he was aware of was that his head ached.

The second thing was that he was strapped down to a very large table with thick leather straps so that he couldn't move, not even his head, and that there was something covering his mouth so that he couldn't speak.

The room was enormous with strong lights above him that blinded him, and he half-closed his eyes against their glare.

Above him, peering down at him, were four people dressed in long green gowns and wearing masks.

'He's awake, Professor,' said the smallest figure, and Ben recognized the voice as that of Hepworth.

The tallest figure nodded and peered closer at him and talked to him through the mask.

'What we're going to do is carbon date you to work out how old you are,' he told Ben.

All you have to do is ask me! thought Ben desperately. I'm 13!

Ben noticed that Hepworth had moved away and had picked up a metal object with a long pointed metal thing sticking out of it. That long pointed metal bit looked like a new version of that drill old Josh the carpenter used. Hepworth switched it on, and the long metal thing began to spin round with a terrible whirring

screaming noise. It was like what old Josh used! It was a drill!

'First, the brain,' said Hepworth, enjoying himself immensely.

Then suddenly the whirring noise stopped. Hepworth looked round, annoyed to see that Crow had switched off the drill at the plug.

'Later, Hepworth,' said Crow. 'You must learn to contain yourself.

'But the brain is the best organ for getting an accurate date on a subject,' protested Hepworth.

'We'll look at his brain later,' said Crow. Turning to one of the other green-covered people, he said: 'First, the fingernails.'

My fingernails! thought Ben in horror, and he began to struggle against the straps. They're going to pull out my fingernails!

But instead the green-gowned assistant took a small clipping from one of Ben's fingernails and took it over to Professor Crow, who was now switching on an electron microscope.

'Hmm,' murmured Crow. 'Well, although there *are* traces of soap here, this is definitely dirt.'

'I think we ought to have a look at his brain before we go much further,' urged Hepworth. 'After all, if anything should happen to him before we take it out. . . .'

'Oh very well,' said Crow. 'If you must. But just a small amount. And don't damage anything else.'

Hepworth nodded happily as he switched on the drill, and once again there was the whirring screaming sound. Ben tensed.

'Hold him down firmly,' Hepworth said to the two other assistants. 'We don't want him moving, it could ruin the drill.'

And the two assistants took hold of Ben's head, holding it in an even firmer grip than the straps that held it to the table, as Hepworth approached the terrified boy, the drill whirring and screaming as he came closer.

Chapter Six

'Wait!'

Crow's voice rang out in the laboratory, and beneath his mask Hepworth's smile vanished. He switched the drill off.

'Come here and look at this! All of you!'

The disappointed Hepworth laid the drill down, and he and the two assistants moved over to where Crow was looking excitedly into the electron microscope.

'This is astonishing!' exclaimed Crow. 'This virus was believed to have died out at the start of this century! This is going to make my career! A Nobel prize at last!'

It was then that Ben noticed that another green-gowned and masked figure had come into the room and was creeping towards the table on tiptoe. As Ben looked, this person pulled down the mask briefly, and he saw it was BB. She put her finger to her lips to keep him silent, though Ben reflected that, with this thing over his mouth, he couldn't make any noise anyway.

As BB crept towards Ben she produced a long thin knife. Oh no! thought Ben. She wants to be the first one to cut me up! But instead she placed the knife against the leather straps that held Ben's legs, and sliced.

She turned and looked at Crow, Hepworth and the two other assistants as they took turns to look at Ben's fingernail clipping under the electron microscope. So far so good. She placed the surgical blade against the leather strap that pinioned Ben's arms, and sliced again.

Crow was once again studying the magnified dirt under the electron microscope, a look of awe in his eyes.

'Who knows what other germs we may find when we open him up?' said Hepworth, eager to return to the part he enjoyed most.

Crow nodded, thoughtfully.

'The bloodstream and the lungs might be a good place to start.'

Hepworth nodded gleefully.

'The bloodstream and the lungs!' he echoed cheerfully, and he nudged the two assistants. 'Right, let's get to work!'

All four of them turned towards the table, and then stopped, gaping open-mouthed in astonishment. The operating table was empty. Crow was the first to find his voice.

'Miller!' he bellowed.

And he strode to a red button on the wall marked 'Alarm', and hit it.

* * *

BB and Ben were walking along the corridor, doing their best not to look suspicious as they headed for one of the fire exits, when the alarm siren went off.

'Run!' yelled BB, and she grabbed the startled Ben's hand and broke into a frantic gallop for the fire door.

But even as she did so she saw that she was too late: a steel shutter was coming down over the fire door, sealing it off. The same would be happening to every exit from the building. They were trapped!

And then an idea struck her, so outrageous, so incredible that she could scarcely believe she had

45

actually thought it! If she couldn't get the boy out in this dimension, then why not get him out the way he had come in, through time! The repairs she had carried out to her time machine might work. No, not 'might', *should*. That sounded better.

She pointed towards the emergency stairs that led down to the basement.

'Quick! To my lab!'

Then she and Ben were hurtling down the stairs, determined to get to the safety of BB's lab before Crow and Hepworth arrived.

* * *

As they ran into BB's lab and BB slammed and locked the steel door shut, Ben stopped to think clearly for the first time.

'What are we doing in here?' he demanded. 'We can't get out of here.'

'Not by the normal methods, no,' agreed BB.

She looked at the time machine, still broken and distorted. She'd repaired the black box and the other components, but the time machine itself was a problem.

'They'll find us here!' persisted Ben.

It was as BB looked at the connections she'd made between the black box and the motorbike that the way round the problem occurred to her. If she arranged it so that the energy field was located around the motorbike itself, with the black box energy amplifier fixed to the pillion. . . !

She set to work, unscrewing the black box from the base of the time machine, while Ben watched her.

'What are you doing?' he asked.

'I'm getting us our way out,' she said.

She placed the black box on the pillion of the bike and began to screw it to the metal brackets at the back. Ben's mouth dropped open as he realized what she had in mind.

'On that?!' he said incredulously.

'It should work,' said BB. 'The theory is still the same.'

'If you think I'm getting on that thing. . . !' snorted Ben scornfully.

Then they heard Crow's voice calling to them over the intercom that connected the lab with the basement corridor outside.

'Dr Miller! We know you're in there! Open this door at once or we shall cut it open! I have ordered the oxy-acetylene equipment and it's on its way.'

'That's the choice you face,' BB pointed out. 'Him and his operating theatre, or me and this machine.'

Ben gulped.

'There is no way out!' called Crow. 'The whole building is sealed! Open this door and hand over the boy, and I shall forget your insubordination!'

BB worked faster. Only a few more nuts to tighten and the black box should be secure.

'Quick! Give me that Number 5 spanner!' she said.

Ben looked around, baffled.

'What's a spanner?' he asked.

BB leapt up, grabbed the spanner she needed, and returned to tightening the nuts.

Outside in the basement corridor Crow turned to Hepworth and the other two assistants who'd just arrived, bringing with them the oxy-acetylene cutting equipment.

'Cut the lock off,' he ordered.

One of the men put on his darkened safety goggles,

lit up the cutting torch, and then set to work, aiming the flame at the door.

Inside the lab Ben leapt back in horror as the blue flame appeared, slicing through the metal.

'They're burning us out!' he yelled.

BB looked and realized what was happening.

'I've finished here,' she said.

She jumped astride the bike and began to punch in the target date on the Time Unit/VDU Display, but the VDU display was dead.

'I can't set the date!' she groaned in anguish. 'We could end up anywhere.'

At the door the blue flame continued to slice its way along, now having cut one side of the lock.

'I'm gonna end up in the graveyard if we don't do something soon,' said Ben.

BB started the bike up.

'OK,' she said. 'Get on!'

And she put her crash helmet on her head, and then held out her second helmet to Ben. Ben looked at it fearfully.

'Wassat for?'

'Safety,' said BB.

'Safety?' repeated Ben. 'You mean this thing ain't safe?' And he backed away.

'What are you doing?' snapped BB. 'Get on!'

'It'll never work! We'll be killed!'

'Would you rather stay here?' demanded BB, and she pointed to the blue flame cutting around the lock of the metal door, which even now was on its last straight stretch.

Ben hesitated, then he jumped on the bike behind BB, and BB pushed the helmet over his head.

'Get ready,' she said.

The next second the blue flame completed its task. The lock fell inward, and the metal door swung open, revealing Crow, Hepworth and the two other technicians in the doorway. Crow glared at BB and Ben triumphantly.

'Get them!' he ordered.

The four men moved into the laboratory as BB put the bike into gear and shot forward, straight at them. The mouths of the four men dropped open, then they threw themselves aside in a frantic scramble to get out of the way as BB and Ben raced out of the lab and into the corridor. BB screeched into a turn, and then accelerated down the corridor, heading straight for a brick wall at the far end, Ben clinging on to her, his eyes closed in terror.

'Here goes!' said BB, and she reached forward and pressed the 'Time Unit' button on the handlebars . . .

Chapter Seven

There was a heart-stopping moment when, for what seemed like an eternity, nothing happened and the bike continued to head straight towards the brick wall. Then blue flashes began to spark off the bike, and off BB and Ben, and just as they were about to hit the wall ahead, it seemed to fold in on itself, and for a split second BB and Ben and the bike folded in on themselves, too, as if they were being turned inside out.

The next second they were back on the bike but in a tunnel of lights, racing along at an incredible speed, but at the same time seeming to be going nowhere, or possibly even backwards, it was impossible to tell.

Then a patch of black suddenly appeared in front of them in the tunnel, black dotted with small glinting spots of white, and they hurtled forward, sailing into nothingness . . .

BB and Ben felt an awful falling sensation. So this is what it's like to travel in time, thought BB, before she realized that she was actually falling. The bike had materialized in the middle of a night sky and was now plummeting to earth. Oh no! she thought. To come all this way and get smashed to bits. . . !

Then something large was looming up beneath them, something large and . . .

Crashwooooshwooshhhswissshhhhcrumppthumppp!!!!!!

The something large had been a farm cart loaded with straw. The cart collapsed under the force of the bike hitting it, and BB and Ben found themselves rolling across damp earthy ground with straw falling down all around them.

BB was the first to stagger to her feet, picking straw from her clothes and removing her crash helmet.

'Where are we?' asked Ben, stumbling to his feet and looking about him at the darkness.

That darkness was suddenly lit up by small fires in the distance, and there were the sounds of explosions. Then there was a woosh and something blew up near them, showering them with earth and stones.

'Someone's shooting bombs at us!' yelled Ben in alarm.

Desperately, BB shouted out: 'Hello! Don't shoot! We're friends!'

Whoever was doing the shooting either didn't hear her, didn't understand her, or didn't like her, because there was another woosh! even nearer this time, and then BB and Ben found themselves sailing through the air in a cloud of earth.

* * *

When they came to, it was just light. BB opened her eyes groggily. She was lying face down on the damp earth and she ached. Every part of her ached, though whether from the explosion or from lying here on the ground, half-covered by all this earth, she didn't know. Come to that, she didn't even know where she was.

She rolled over, shaking her head to clear the dirt from her eyes, and found herself looking up at a ring of

52

faces staring down at her, a ring of men wearing metal helmets, surprise writ large on every face.

* * *

BB and Ben, their hands tied, stumbled across the uneven ground following a rickety old farm cart pulled by an even older looking horse, a real old English shire. On the cart was BB's motorbike and their crash helmets.

Surrounding BB were the men in the metal helmets, some of them armed with swords, some with long spears, some carrying long rifles. Muskets, BB thought, remembering pictures in history books. From the mens' outfits it looked as if they had arrived back in the middle of the seventeenth century.

This is incredible! she thought. Along with science and her motorbike, history had long been one of her passions. In fact it had been the driving force behind her desire to research time travel. She had spent many hours travelling around looking at old buildings, spending time in museums, but her dream had always been actually to *experience* the events as they happened. And now here she was, doing just that!

Beside her Ben didn't seem to be having as enjoyable a time as BB. As he saw it, here they were, prisoners, surrounded by big men armed with all sorts of weapons. By the look of it they were heading towards the main entrance of a large castle with smoke coming from it, obviously from the battle they had landed in the night before. Whatever was going to happen to them, it didn't look good.

They passed through the stone archway of the main gateway, the large wooden gates creaking shut behind them as the procession arrived on the courtyard of the castle.

The courtyard showed signs of the previous night's battle, smoke still coming from broken walls where cannonballs had crashed through the stones. In the centre of the courtyard a camp was being set up, tents hastily erected. The procession passed what looked like a hospital tent where a surgeon, his arms covered in blood, was cleaning the blade of an old-fashioned saw.

It's a Roundhead camp, realized BB. These are Roundhead soldiers, Oliver Cromwell's army. She nudged Ben.

'You're nearest to the cart,' she said. 'See if you can see the screen on the front of the bike. See if it's working and what numbers are on it.'

Ben nodded and craned his neck up.

'A one and a six and a four and a five,' he whispered.

BB smiled, pleased at her recognition of the events around her.

'1645!' she whispered triumphantly. 'We're in the middle of the English Civil War!' And she looked around her in awe as they followed the trundling cart out of the first courtyard and into an inner courtyard, a smaller one. She shook her head, still wondering at it all. 'This is just fabulous!'

Ben looked at her, open-mouthed. Fabulous! Here they were, caught up in a war, tied up like this, and she thought it was 'fabulous'?! Inwardly he groaned. Just his luck to travel in time with an idiot!

'What happened in this war?' he whispered, one eye on the grim-faced soldiers on either side of them.

'There was a revolution and Oliver Cromwell and his men, the Roundheads, wanted to get rid of the king.

The other side, the Royalists, wanted to keep the king,' BB answered, speaking out of the corner of her mouth, which made it difficult for Ben to hear her properly. However, he got the general idea.

'Who won?' he asked, thinking that it would be nice to know if they'd been captured by the winning or the losing side.

Before BB could answer the cart rumbled to a halt and the whole procession stopped.

The captain of the guard came from the front of the procession back to BB and Ben, pulling out a knife as he did so. BB flinched back, but all he did was cut the ropes that bound their wrists. Behind him two soldiers were manhandling the motorbike, trying to get it down from the cart.

'Please take good care with that,' said BB. 'I know you don't understand about motorcycles yet, but . . .'

The captain pushed her roughly towards an open door that led into the castle.

'Hold your tongue!' he growled.

BB bridled.

'There's no need to be rough,' she objected. 'I do know that in a war prisoners have rights.'

The captain gestured to two of the soldiers to take hold of BB and Ben, and they found themselves pushed roughly in through the open door, and down a stone passageway into the heart of the castle.

They were obviously heading towards a half-open door at the far end of the passage. As they approached the door they heard a blood-curdling scream from the room within. Ben froze. It was a torture chamber! They were going to be tortured!

BB interpreted the scream differently. She turned to the captain of the guard, concerned.

'Is someone in trouble? I'm a doctor. That is, I have a doctorate in Quantum Physics, but. . . .'

The captain didn't answer, merely gestured to the two soldiers to push BB and Ben in through the doorway into the room.

The room, like the rest of the castle, showed the signs of battle, with scorched walls, and broken windows.

It was a large room. At the far end a big man sat in a chair. On either side of him stood two armed soldiers. Kneeling on top of the big man, facing him was a much smaller man and he seemed to be doing something horrible to the big man's face, because as the small man's arm moved sharply, they heard the scream again, obviously coming from the man in the chair.

BB turned her face away, unable to look at whatever horrible torture was going on in this room. Whatever it was, she knew that they were next!

Chapter Eight

Ben had no such scruples and he watched in fascinated horror as the small man climbed down off the big man. In his hand the small man held a pair of pliers, and in the jaw of the pliers was a large tooth.

'There's one at the back needs to come out as well, but we'll leave that for another time,' said the small man, and he put the tooth down on a table.

A dentist! realized Ben. The small man was a dentist!

The big man stood up, rubbing his jaw. Now he was standing up, BB and Ben could see just how big he was. It wasn't just that he was tall, he was wide, and very muscular.

'Master Leather Hardbones will see you now,' the captain growled at BB and Ben.

The big man, Leather Hardbones, stretched after his ordeal in the chair. BB and Ben could almost hear his muscles crack as he flexed them. The dentist had already taken his leave, off to the courtyard to offer his services to the surgeon.

Ben gulped as the huge figure of Hardbones approached them with a slow menacing walk.

'Great idea of yours, getting away from that Professor bloke,' he whispered sarcastically. 'We could have been in serious trouble.'

'Leave this to me,' said BB confidently. 'I know how to handle this.'

The captain slapped the riding crop he was carrying against his leg.

'Silence!' he bellowed.

Hardbones surveyed BB and Ben, his gaze hard and brutal.

'So!' he grinned nastily, his grin showing blackened and broken teeth. 'More bodies!'

BB held up her hand, like a child in class.

'Excuse me,' she said. 'May I say a word?'

Everyone stared at her, astonished at this effrontery. Too astonished, in fact, to stop her as she continued: 'There's a very simple explanation for our being here. We have come from the future.'

Ben groaned silently to himself, while the Roundheads exchanged baffled glances. Come from the future?

'We came on that thing outside,' added BB. 'It's called a motorcycle. If I show you how it works I'm sure you'll agree. . . .'

Hardbones seemed to recover his powers of speech and movement.

'Quiet!' he roared, the force of his anger making BB sway back.

Then Hardbones noticed the captain gesturing to him, and he and the captain moved to one side, out of earshot of the prisoners and the other soldiers.

'It is truly a strange device, Master Hardbones,' murmured the captain. 'It might be to our advantage to let the woman show us how it works. It could be some ingenious war machine and useful to us.'

Hardbones nodded thoughtfully.

BB and Ben watched the two men tensely, and watched Hardbones nodding as the captain continued to whisper.

'I think he's gonna go for it,' Ben whispered to BB. 'And if they do, as soon as you get it started. . . .'

'I know,' nodded BB as she whispered back: 'It'll prove to them I'm telling the truth.'

Ben gaped at her, astonished. BB looked at Ben, puzzled by the expression on his face.

'What's the matter?' she asked.

'Don't you realize they are going to kill us?' whispered Ben to her.'

'Of course they're not,' scoffed BB. 'We're prisoners of war . . .'

Then her voice trailed off as she saw the evil smile on Hardbones's face as the captain finished whispering, and she gulped. Maybe Ben was right. Maybe these people didn't play by the rules.

Hardbones and the captain returned to BB and Ben.

'I've made my mind up,' said Hardbones. 'You can show us how this device works.'

BB hesitated momentarily, then she nodded. Once she and Ben were on the bike it would be a simple matter to escape. If they couldn't make it through the doors, then they could always use the bike as a time machine again and escape that way. Hardbones gestured to BB to follow him. As she did so, Ben also stepped forward, but was stopped by the captain.

'Where d'you think you're going?' he demanded.

Ben shot a look of appeal at BB.

'He's — er — he's part of it,' said BB quickly. 'It won't work without him.'

The captain and Hardbones exchanged quizzical looks, then Hardbones nodded.

'All right, bring the boy,' he growled. 'But if you're lying it'll be the worse for you . . .'

BB and Ben followed Hardbones and the captain out of the room and along the passage, back the way they had come, out into the inner courtyard.

As they walked, BB tried to strike up pleasant conversation to disarm their captors: 'I suppose the internal combustion engine is quite a new idea for you. . . ,' she began.

'Silence!' growled Hardbones.

And so is politeness, thought BB acidly.

Outside in the courtyard the motorbike was leaning against the cart on which it had been brought to the castle. A small group of soldiers were gathered around the motorbike, poking it with puzzled expressions on their faces as they tried to work out what it was and what it did.

'Attention!' shouted the captain, and the men sprang into rigid postures of attention and saluted.

'Bring that thing here!' ordered Hardbones.

The soldiers took hold of the bike and wheeled it clumsily towards Hardbones.

'Right,' said Hardbones to BB. 'Show us.'

BB took the bike from the soldiers and sat astride it.

'This machine has a 750cc engine,' she said by way of introduction, like a lecturer addressing a class. 'The earlier models had kick-start ignition, but this is automatic.

And she turned the ignition key and the bike roared into life. The effect on the Roundheads was electrifying. They backed away from the bike as if it were going to explode. When it didn't, they turned their attention back to looking at it, all still feeling slightly unnerved.

BB walked calmly over to the cart where the crash helmets lay. She picked them up, addressing the Roundheads the whole while: 'The motorcycle is driven by an internal combustion engine, in which the motion of the piston is converted into rotary motion by the principle of the crank.'

She walked back to the bike, placed one of the crash helmets on the pillion, and slipped the other on her head, explaining:

'These are called crash helmets. These are essential wear if you're going to follow the safety code.'

She gestured for Ben to join her.

'This is where my young assistant takes up his very important role.

With that Ben sauntered over to BB, not too fast because he didn't want to arouse the Roundheads' suspicions. BB fixed the helmet on Ben's head, and then Ben climbed on the bike behind her and put his arms around her waist. BB continued her lecture in matter-of-fact tones:

'To make the bike move you put it into gear,' and as she said this she pulled in the clutch lever and slipped it into first gear, 'and then you let out the clutch . . .'

As the bike hurtled forward the Roundheads yelled in fear and jumped back in confusion. BB took the opportunity to head the bike for the outer courtyard. Through there was the main gate. If the gates were open then they would be free!

Hardbones was the first to recover from the initial shock.

'They're getting away! After them!'

The Roundhead soldiers, led by Hardbones and the captain, chased after the escaping BB and Ben, through the short passageways to the outer courtyard.

In the outer courtyard the motorcycle was causing chaos and havoc. The Roundheads had never seen anything like this fiery noisy machine before and they ran to escape from it, crashing into tent poles in their attempts to escape, bringing tents crashing down.

BB weaved her way through the chaos towards the main gates, but they were shut!

'We can't get out!' yelled Ben.

'Don't worry, we'll get out the way we came in!' said BB. 'Through time!'

The Roundhead soldiers had recovered now, egged on by Hardbones and the captain who had arrived in the outer courtyard, swords drawn and swearing at BB and Ben.

'I need a straight run so I can get up speed,' said BB.

'Up there!' pointed Ben, and BB looked at where he was pointing. Yes, he was right, some short steps went up to a long parapet along the castle wall. That should be a long enough distance to get the revs up to the right power.

BB headed the bike up the short steps, scattering soldiers in her path.

Behind her she could hear the sound of muskets being fired and bullets ricocheted off the stone walls around her. They were being shot at!

She was on the parapet now. At the far end was a gap in a wall which looked as if it just went out into empty space. It was now or never.

'Hold on!' she said to Ben, and she pulled open the accelerator and the bike hurtled along the parapet, heading for the empty gate in the wall. BB pressed the 'Time Unit' button on the handlebars. Nearer and nearer they headed for the gap in the wall. Ben looked over BB's shoulder at the approaching gap, with just empty space beyond.

'We're getting a bit close,' he said, worried.

'Don't worry,' said BB. 'It'll be like it was before. It'll work at the last minute.

Nervously Ben turned to see where the pursuing soldiers were, and it was then he noticed the leads trailing uselessly from the black box on the pillion of the bike. The Time Unit wasn't connected! They were heading off the edge of the castle wall into empty space!

Chapter Nine

'Aaaarghhhhh!!' yelled BB and Ben together as once more they fell through empty air on the motorbike — only this time there was no cart laden with straw to break their fall, just a dried up moat rushing up to meet them.

Crummmpppp!! The bike hit the ground, bounced, and then BB and Ben were lying on the hollow earth, all the breath knocked out of them.

* * *

Ten minutes later, BB and Ben, aching and bruised from their fall, were being pushed along by angry soldiers. They stumbled, almost falling, through the door of the interrogation room. Leather Hardbones, pacing around the room, looked up as they came in, his face showing anger, and also amazement at what had just happened.

BB forced what she hoped was a cheerful smile. 'And that's how it works!' she said.

Hardbones didn't smile back. He stopped his pacing and approached them, although somewhat hesitantly for such a large and powerful man. The reason for his hesitancy become apparent when he growled in low tones: 'Riding a metal horse. Flying through the air. You be a witch!'

Ben shuddered, as did the Roundhead soldiers in the room. A witch!

BB laughed. 'Oh really! There are no such things as witches. That's superstition . . .'

The captain, fuming at the way BB and Ben had almost managed to escape, cracked his riding crop against his leg again.

'Silence when Master Hardbones speaks!' he bellowed.

BB looked at him, concerned.

'Don't you ever hurt yourself doing that?' she asked.

'Do you deny that you be a witch?' demanded Hardbones.

'Of course I deny it!' said BB stoutly. 'Look, I know this all sounds pretty incredible, but we really are from the future. I'm from the twentieth century and he's from the nineteenth.'

This further information only made the Roundhead soldiers in the room gape more, while Hardbones and the Roundhead captain looked at each other with a mixture of suspicion, anger, and deep concern. Suspicion and anger because this woman could be a Royalist spy, and deep concern in case she was really a witch and was capable of terrifying deeds. Certainly they had seen her riding through the air on this metal horse.

'I'll prove it to you,' said BB, and her face creased into a frown as she tried to think of some knowledge that she might have that would prove to these people that she really *had* come from the future. '1645, English History. What happened apart from this Civil War?' It had to be something happening *now* that only someone in the future could know. Then an idea struck her. 'Got it! Sir Isaac Newton! Born 1642!'

Hardbones and the captain looked at BB bewildered. What was she going on about now? Was this some spell, some incantation?

BB looked at them and saw the blankness of their expressions. Why couldn't they see what she was getting at?

'Sir Isaac Newton!' she said desperately. 'One of history's greatest scientists! The man who's going to discover gravity!'

'I think the woman be mad,' she heard the captain murmur to Hardbones. 'Maybe possessed.'

'At this very moment he's three years old!' said BB. 'Check it! Call the Registrar of Births or whoever's in charge of that sort of thing.'

Next to BB, Ben groaned, aware of the impression that she was creating and seeing from the faces of the Roundheads that with every word BB accused herself of either madness or witchcraft.

'All right, let's try another one!' said BB, her tone growing more desperate. 'Any of you people ever heard of Rembrandt, the Dutch painter? He's painting pictures around about now.'

It was obvious from the expressions on the faces around her that the name of Rembrandt didn't strike any chords.

'There's obviously not much education in these times,' snapped BB, feeling frustrated at being sur-rounded by all this ignorance. 'Look, it might be a good idea if I spoke to the person at the top. Your boss. Who's in charge here?'

'I am,' growled Hardbones.

'Ah,' said BB, thinking to herself: well that doesn't help me much.

'I think this calls for the attention of the Witchfinder General, Master Hardbones,' the captain murmured to Hardbones in a low voice. Hardbones glared at the captain, put out. This man was always doing this to him, coming up with ideas! Just because the captain had been a clerk of some sort before this revolution and could read and write, while he, Leather Hardbones, had been a blacksmith, the captain thought it gave him some sort of superiority. Huh! After this war was won he'd show the captain what he thought of jumped-up clerks.

'*I* was about to suggest that!' he snapped. 'You're not the only one with ideas, you know.' To BB and Ben he announced in official, almost pompous, tones: 'You shall be locked up and tomorrow you shall be brought before the Witchfinder General, Matthew Hopkins. Take them away!'

As BB and Ben found themselves being hustled roughly out of the door by the captain and the soldiers, BB tried one last appeal to Hardbones: 'I am not a witch! I am just a perfectly ordinary researcher into time travel. . . !'

But the door slammed shut, and BB and Ben were shoved along a passage and towards some stone stairs that led down to the castle dungeons.

Below ground, the passages were damp, black water dripping down the stones of the walls. The stench from the cells was indescribable. Obviously people had been locked up here for weeks without any proper sanitation. As they passed the barred doors BB and Ben saw people chained to walls or lying down on the straw-covered floors. As the Roundheads had only taken the castle the previous night, these were obviously the previous occupants of the castle, the Royalists, now awaiting their fate.

At one point Ben slipped in a puddle on the floor and fell against one of the soldiers accompanying them, but was soon pushed forward again, with a blow to the back of his head to tell him to be more careful.

They stopped at a barred door and the captain of the guard unlocked the door and stood aside to let BB and Ben enter the cell.

'Get in there, witch!' ordered the captain.

BB and Ben stepped in, and at once the door clanged shut behind them, the captain locking it. They watched through the bars as the captain and the soldiers made their way back along the passage towards the stairs. Then they turned and took stock of their situation.

There were four prisoners already in the cell, three men and one woman, their clothes torn and grimy and their faces and bodies bruised and marked. When BB and Ben had entered they had been lying on the straw strewn around the floor, but now they were all moving back carefully away from BB towards the wall, fear and suspicion in their eyes, the woman crossing herself. BB decided that she needed to address them to set the matter straight.

'Look, about what that soldier said just now about me being a witch, I feel it's important that I set things straight. I'm not a witch.'

At her words there was a slight feeling of a lessening of fear in the cell from the four other prisoners.

'I've come from three hundred and sixty years in the future, with this boy here.'

Any lessening of fear instantly ceased as the prisoners cowered back again from BB, the woman once more crossing herself and muttering 'witch' under her breath, and two of the men tapping their heads to each other to indicate that they felt that perhaps BB was just mad.

BB didn't notice all this. She smiled at the four prisoners.

'I feel it's important you know this so that you don't get the wrong impression of me. All right?'

BB then sat down on the straw next to Ben. 'I think that's eased the situation a little,' she told him confidently. Ben looked at BB and shook his head at her naivety. Then he asked her, in low tones because he didn't want to arouse suspicions about *him* among the other people in the cell: 'What do you know about this Hopkins bloke, this Witchfinder General?'

BB thought it over, trying to remember what she had been taught in school about the Civil War and the seventeenth century witch-hunts.

'From what I can remember, the Witchfinder General was a fairly terrifying man who went around England smelling out witches.'

'Smelling them?'

BB nodded.

'Luckily I had a bath yesterday,' she said.

Ben didn't laugh. 'And what happened when he smelt a witch?' he asked.

'The witch was burnt at the stake,' said BB, suddenly not happy at the thought.

Ben shivered as if a cold draught had blown through the cell. Burnt at the stake!

'Did they have boy witches?' he asked nervously.

'No,' said BB. 'As far as I remember they were all women. A pretty obvious case of discrimination. Anyway, once this Witchfinder General gets here tomorrow we'll be all right. He'll see I'm not a witch.'

'The Witchfinder General *always* finds witches,' said the woman prisoner, who had been listening to all this.

'Always?' said BB, surprised. 'That good, is he?'

'Everyone that he investigates confesses. And then their souls are saved.'

'That's clever,' murmured BB. 'How does he do that?'

There was an awkward silence in the cell, then one of the men spoke up: 'By burning them.'

And the other prisoners nodded in unhappy agreement.

'But why on earth do they confess. . . ?' said BB, shocked. Then the realization struck her, and she gulped. 'Let me guess. Torture?'

'The rack,' said the woman prisoner sombrely. 'The red hot irons.'

BB shuddered at the thought. Torture!

'What do they do to friends of witches?' asked Ben, not too happy about the way this conversation was leading.

'Sometimes they burn them,' said one of the men. 'Sometimes they chop their heads off.'

'Do they ever just feed them and let them go?' asked Ben hopefully.

One look at the sombre expressions on the faces of the prisoners was enough to tell Ben that the answer to his question was a firm 'No'. BB and Ben exchanged fearful looks. They were in a terrible predicament, and their future looked like being miserably short, cut off by fire.

Chapter Ten

That night as darkness fell, BB tried to sleep, but every time she closed her eyes all she could see was herself tied to a stake with bales of straw stacked up around her and someone about to set light to them. Eventually she must have dozed off because she found herself being woken as someone shook her shoulder.

She opened her eyes and sat up on the straw.

'Wha. . . ?' she began, then fell silent as she saw that it was Ben, his finger pressed to his lips to quieten her. Ben looked carefully around the cell at the other four prisoners, all apparently fast asleep, two of the men even snoring, then he dipped his hand into his pocket and pulled out a large key.

BB's eyes widened in astonishment.

'Where. . . ?' she began, but Ben shushed her again, and she lowered her voice to a whisper: 'Where did you get that?'

'When I bumped into that guard,' whispered back Ben.

'Why didn't you say anything before?'

'Because we don't know if we can trust these people in here,' whispered Ben, and he turned to indicate the other prisoners, and found all four of them wide awake watching them. Ben gulped.

'You were going to escape and leave us here,' growled one of the men accusingly.

'No. . . ,' lied Ben nervously.

'No he wasn't,' said BB, leaping to Ben's defence. 'I can vouch for this boy. He is loyal honest and clean.' Then she thought about it. 'Well, he's clean.' Then she looked at Ben, bruised and grimy and filthy from their recent adventures. 'He *was* clean.'

'You'd never get out on your own,' said another of the men. 'There are guards out there. But if we go together we stand more chance.'

'That makes sense,' nodded BB. Turning to Ben she said: 'Are you sure this is the right key?'

'I hope so,' said Ben. 'It was the only one I could grab.'

Ben moved swiftly to the bars of the door, looked along the dank passageway, lit by flaming torches, to check that no-one was around, then inserted the key into the lock, and turned it. Only it didn't turn.

'It's the wrong key!' groaned the woman prisoner.

'Wait!' said BB, determined not to give up so easily. 'Try it the other way.'

Ben turned the key the other way, and as they watched, it turned. There was a click . . . and the door swung open!

The prisoners looked at one another in delight and clapped Ben heartily on the back in congratulation. Then, with one of the men prisoners leading the way, they crept along the damp passageway, heading for the stairs.

* * *

For his part, Leather Hardbones had been unable to sleep, because of the terrible agonies from his aching tooth.

Maybe he should have had it taken out, but the

dentist had gone for the night and would not be back until the morning. Then a thought struck him. The witch, she would deal in herbs and potions, maybe she would have something that could ease the pain. Maybe he would offer her something to help her ease his pain: death before being burnt for example.

It was with these thoughts, and with a severely aching tooth, that Hardbones clumped down the stone steps that led to the cells. As he turned the corner into the dampness of the passageway he thought he heard a movement, and then he saw that he had indeed heard something because he came face to face with a man covered in grime, straw sticking out of his clothes, and behind the man were at least five others. With a shock Hardbones realized what was going on. He drew his sword, at the same time shouting out: 'Escape! Escape. . . !'

A hard punch full in his face from the grimy prisoner stopped Hardbones in mid-speech, and the Roundhead commander crashed to the stone floor, unconscious. But too late, his shout of alarm had alerted the guards elsewhere in the castle, and even now there were the sounds of soldiers rushing about, swords being drawn, muskets being made ready.

'We'll have to fight our way out!' said the prisoner at the front, and with that he grabbed up Hardbones's sword and charged up the stone steps, the others following close behind.

By the time they reached the ground floor passage three soldiers had appeared to answer Hardbones's shout of alarm. However, thanks to the suddenness of the escape, and the ferocity of the prisoners who fought with the desperation of people fighting for their lives, the prisoners were able to batter the soldiers back, forcing them towards the door that led to the small inner courtyard. As the prisoners fought, knocking down and overpowering the three soldiers, they snatched up their weapons and rushed out into the courtyard.

Here it was a different situation. The courtyard was lit by flaming torches on the outside walls of the castle buildings and by burning braziers, the sentries on duty were alert, and as the prisoners spilled out from the main door they found themselves facing a heavily armed force of Roundheads.

'At them!' shouted the leading prisoner, and the four prisoners set to, laying about them with pikes and swords, kicking over the burning braziers, spilling hot coals at the soldiers and forcing them back.

Ben grabbed BB's arm.

'Let's find that thing of yours and get out of here!' he shouted in her ear.

BB nodded, and under the confusion of the battle in the courtyard, they crept along the side of the castle building, keeping to the shadows of the stone walls as they moved from buttress to buttress.

A row of small outbuildings lay ahead of them, looking like stables.

'Let's try there,' suggested BB. 'They think it's a flying horse, that might be where they'd keep it.'

Behind them the fighting continued with a fierceness that terrified BB. In the light of the burning braziers and the torches, she saw swords rise and fall, saw soldiers topple, blood coming from gashes on their faces, saw the woman prisoner laying about her with a stout staff as the prisoners struggled to get to the main courtyard. Almost in spite of herself, she found herself muttering in awe: 'They'll never believe this in Cambridge.'

79

'Come on!' urged Ben.

She followed Ben in a crouching run across the courtyard to the outbuildings. Ben moved swiftly from door to door, jumping up at each one and clinging to the bars of the door's small window long enough to peer in and see what was inside. At the third door he found it. The motorbike gleamed dimly in the half-light, lying on its side in the outbuilding on bales of straw.

Ben dropped down from the barred window and gave BB a confident grin.

'Found it!' he said.

He pulled at the door, but it was locked.

'Let me have a go,' said BB, and she took hold of the handle and pulled, straining back as hard as she could, but it was no use. The door was locked as firmly as any door could be.

'We're going to have to try to break it down,' said Ben.

BB looked at the door doubtfully. It appeared pretty solid to her. However, if it was the only way . . .

She was just about to crash her shoulder against it, when a shout behind her made her turn round.

'There they are!'

Leather Hardbones stood in the centre of the courtyard, his whole huge frame glowing red from the burning fires, a malevolent finger pointing directly at them.

'Whoops!' said Ben.

'Maybe we can try explaining. . . ?' gulped BB hopefully to Ben, but Ben was already running, and so were a whole load of Roundhead soldiers, swords drawn, angry expressions on their faces, charging straight for her.

'Wait for me!' she bellowed, and then she was running after Ben, not knowing where the boy was going but trusting that his instinct for self-preservation would lead them to safety.

Ben just ran. Behind him he could hear BB, and behind her a whole troop of shouting and yelling Roundhead soldiers, their armour clanking as they ran.

Ahead of him was an open doorway into the castle building. Ben dived through, and found himself by a circular stone stairway that went up.

He hesitated just a second, then, almost without realizing it, he found himself running up, up, up, his feet beating on the stone steps. Behind him he could hear BB panting, and behind her the heavier thud thud thud of the soldiers' boots.

He could also hear Hardbones urging the soldiers on with bloodcurdling cries of: 'Take them alive! I want to burn them! I want to disembowel them!'

Then Ben found himself at the top of the stairs and out in the night sky. BB came hurtling out of the staircase and nearly crashed into him, but he hurled himself back against her and stood for a second, clinging to her, shaking. BB edged forward and saw why. Their flight had brought them out on to a ledge which seemed to go nowhere. Below them was just darkness. In the moonlight BB could dimly make out reflections on fast-moving water. About a hundred metres below, a river curled its way past the castle.

A hundred metres!

BB closed her eyes and pulled back from the edge of the ledge.

Behind them the soldiers were nearly at the top of the stairs now, Hardbones's shouts getting nearer:

'Don't kill them! I shall boil their eyes! I shall tear the flesh from their bones! They will plead to be burnt!'

81

BB and Ben looked at one another, gripping hands, their faces terrified. BB gulped.

'Let's go for it!' she said.

Then she and Ben ran towards the edge of the ledge, just as the soldiers appeared in the doorway from the staircase. As the soldiers watched, BB and Ben hurled themselves out into the empty dark space and plummeted towards the river far below.

Chapter Eleven

It was the sound of birds that woke BB. The dawn chorus was chattering and singing as the first streaks of daylight lit the night sky filling the east with streaks of pale blue and orange and red from the rising sun.

BB opened her eyes. She was lying on a mixture of sand and clay, her legs trailing in the marshy ground that marked the edge of a river.

The river! Of course!

She was about to get up, then she stopped. Better check first to see if anything was broken. Cautiously she tensed her muscles. Everything seemed all right, although she felt stiff. She ran her hands over her body, pressing her ribs and legs gently, checking for broken bones.

No, she seemed OK. So far so good.

She saw Ben lying face down a short distance away, his feet trailing in the running water of the river. As she watched, he stirred into consciousness, and she staggered to her feet and went over to him.

Ben sat up, shaking his head and looking about him in bewilderment.

'What happened?!' he asked, dazed.

'We survived,' said BB.

She still couldn't get over it. A jump like that! They had been lucky, the river might have been only a few centimetres deep with rocks at the bottom. As it had turned out, it had obviously carried them downriver for some way, because there was no sight of the castle. Which didn't mean that they weren't still near it because around them, lining the banks of the river, were trees which stopped them seeing very far. They had obviously been washed up on a bend where the river ran through a small wood.

Ben had dragged himself out of the water and now he and BB were standing up, wringing out their clothes.

'I think we'll dry off faster if we walk,' said BB. 'I also think we'll be safer under cover.'

They set off, away from the river, walking deeper into the wood. As they walked BB ran through their situation in her mind. There had to be a simple answer to all this, a simple way to get out of the spot they were in.

'Do you know what I think?' she said.

Ben nodded.

'We gotta get that machine of yours back so we can get out of here,' he said firmly.

'We've got to get my machine back so that we can get out of here,' BB told him.

Ben looked at her.

'I just said that! I thought you were supposed to be clever.'

'The problem is: how do we get it back?'

'Nick it,' said Ben.

BB shook her head.

'Out of the question. What we have to do is to talk to them. *Persuade* them to give it back to us.'

Ben looked at her as if she was mad.

'They tried to kill us!' he pointed out.

'That's because the Roundheads think we're on the other side, the Cavaliers. You know, all fluffy hats and silk suits and stuff. All we have to do is persuade the Roundheads that we're on *their* side and we'll be OK!'

The sound of a twig breaking behind some tall bushes nearby made them both stop and look around at the wood tensely.

'Who d'you reckon that is?' whispered Ben.

'It must be the Roundheads,' said BB.

'It could be that other lot' pointed out Ben.

BB gave him a confident smile.

'Trust me. I have a feeling about this.' And then she shouted out: 'Long live the Roundheads!'

At her shout the bushes beside them parted and into view, swords drawn and muskets levelled, stepped a party of men, all looking grimly at them, and all dressed in clothes that showed them to be Royalists.

As BB and Ben discovered on the walk back, the men with the guns and swords were all servants at nearby Chalmerston Manor and had been out on a hunting party as a result of rumours of Roundheads in the area preparing to launch an attack on the manor. The discovery of BB and Ben in the wood, especially BB's incriminating shout, had led the pair to be chained securely together, and then led under armed escort to the manor itself, a distance of some three miles.

Chalmerston Manor was a huge mansion, red bricks and leaded windows glinting in the sun. As they entered the yard in front of the manor house, a servant boy appeared from round the back of the house with four snarling dogs on two leashes. The boy was obviously having difficulty controlling the dogs. As the dogs saw the party approach they strained at the leashes, lips pulled back to show sharp teeth. Ben gulped.

'They don't look very friendly.' he said.

'Don't worry,' said BB. 'The trick in handling dogs is not to let them see you're afraid.'

Suddenly the dogs charged forward, momentarily dragging the boy off balance, and BB moved swiftly to hide behind Ben, who then tried to hide behind BB. The leader of the party, who BB had heard called by the name of Matlock and who was armed with a rifle, snapped out an order and the dogs stopped in their tracks, although they continued to growl.

'Is that how you do it?' Ben said sarcastically to BB.

'I was just composing myself,' lied BB.

'Get those dogs to the kennels!' Matlock ordered the boy.

The boy nodded and hauled the leashes, pulling the dogs in the direction of the stables.

'You others, get about your duties,' continued Matlock. 'I'll take these two to the master.'

The other servants dutifully disappeared, with suspicious glances at BB and Ben, while Matlock gestured with the barrel of the rifle towards the back of the manor house.

'On!' snapped Matlock.

BB and Ben trudged on, Matlock's gaze fixed firmly on them, his finger resting ominously on the trigger of the rifle.

Under Matlock's surly directions they found themselves walking through a small door at the back of the large mansion, and into a kitchen where three servants were bustling about preparing desserts of jellies and cakes. all of which Ben eyed hungrily. It seemed to him ages since he had last eaten.

Matlock had stopped momentarily and was frowning at a bowl containing pieces of meat, obviously scraps and offal.

'That should have been given to the dogs this morning!' he said sternly. 'Every morning at dawn! Or d'you want them eating *you*?'

The chastened servants lowered their eyes. Matlock was about to move on when he spotted Ben's hands reaching for a small cake, and he brought the barrel of the rifle down on Ben's wrist. Ben leapt back with a cry.

'On!' said Matlock.

Obediently BB and Ben trudged on, out of the kitchen, along a short passageway, and then into a banqueting room. The large table was almost groaning under the weight of food upon it: a boar's head, hams, roast turkey, exotic fruits, all manner of vegetables, everything a glutton could desire.

Sitting at the table, picking his way through this enormous feast, was a small thin-faced man dressed (over-dressed, thought BB) in silks and ruffles, a large powdered white wig cascading down from his head to the shoulders of his pink silk jacket.

'Begging your pardon, Lord Chalmerston. . . ,' began Matlock.

Chalmerston looked up, a peevish look on his face.

'Yes? What is it? Can't you see I'm at lunch?'

'Begging your pardon, but we found these two by the river. When we approached them they shouted: "Long live the Roundheads!" '

Ben glared at BB.

'It was a mistake anyone could have made,' BB whispered defensively.

'Obviously Roundhead spies,' said Chalmerston shortly. 'Shoot them.'

With that he returned to his eating. Matlock gave a little bow and poked BB with a rifle.

'Right,' he said. 'Out.'

BB stared at first Matlock, then at Chalmerston, shocked. Shot?!

'You can't shoot us just like that!' she protested.

'Yes I can,' said Chalmerston, and carried on eating.

'We're not Roundhead spies!' BB called desperately, avoiding Matlock's attempts to push her outside. 'We don't even like them! They tried to kill us.'

Ben nodded in fervent agreement, but it was all having little effect on Chalmerston, who waved a hand dismissively at them in a gesture for Matlock to carry out his orders.

'Don't you want to ask us questions first?' pleaded BB, hoping to gain some extra time.'

'No,' said Chalmerston shortly. 'I don't talk to people who shout "Long live the Roundheads".'

'*She* shouted "Long live the Roundheads!"' put in Ben quickly. 'I was gonna shout "Long live the . . ."' And then he stopped and turned to BB, a quizzical expression on his face. 'Who are this lot again?'

BB, stung by this treachery on Ben's part, leapt at him, her hands reaching for his throat to throttle him.

'You little traitor!'

'Get off him!' snarled Matlock, and began to poke her with the rifle barrel.

'What's going on?'

At the sound of the woman's voice from the doorway, all the action suddenly stopped as if frozen. BB let Ben go and they turned to see a tall woman in the doorway, as overdressed as Lord Chalmerston in the Royalist fashion: a huge billowing dress, an enormous powdered wig, and at least three beauty spots (or they may have been moles) on her face.

Lord Chalmerston had stopped eating and he now looked at his much taller wife and forced a sickly smile.

'Hello, my little petal,' he greeted her.

Lady Chalmerston ignored her husband. Instead she strode straight over to BB and Ben and Matlock.

'Matlock, who are these people and what are you doing with them?'

'I was just taking them out to shoot them, milady,' said Matlock.

'Shoot them?!' gasped Lady Chalmerston, shocked.

'Yes, milady,' said Matlock.

Lady Chalmerston, obviously angry at this, turned on her husband, her eyes blazing. Chalmerston, thinking quickly, tried to cover himself and glared at Matlock, switching the blame to the unfortunate servant: 'Shoot them, you fool?!' he snorted, his voice rising at least two octaves. 'I didn't say shoot them, I said . . . I said . . . *Shoo* them!'

Everyone else in the room looked at Chalmerston, bewildered.

'Shoe them, milord?' said the baffled Matlock. 'D'you mean put horseshoes on them?'

'No no! Shoo them . . . Shoo them . . . *Show* them to their rooms.' He forced a sickly grin at his wife. 'The man's obviously going deaf.'

'But you said they was Roundhead spies!' defended Matlock, a note of indignation trembling in his voice, though not enough to suggest that he was openly contradicting his lord and master.

'Nonsense!' snapped Chalmerston. 'I said . . . I said they must have some round mince pies.'

And he picked up a mince pie from the feast on the table to illustrate his point.

Lady Chalmerston nodded and swept round the table to stand behind her husband.

'Absolutely,' she said. 'Take their chains off them, Matlock, then show them to their rooms.' To BB and Ben she said, with a welcoming smile: 'You'll find some lovely clean clothes to choose from. Have a nice rest, then you must join us for dinner.'

The fed-up Matlock grumbled under his breath, but then gestured for BB and Ben to follow him.

'This way,' he said shortly.

BB and Ben gave Lady Chalmerston smiles that stemmed as much from relief as gratitude, and followed Matlock out of the room.

As soon as they had gone, Lady Chalmerston turned on her husband, her smile now gone. In its place was a snarl that sent cold shivers up Lord Chalmerston's spine.

'You idiot!' she snapped. 'Our first guests for months and you were going to shoot them!'

'But we always kill our guests!' protested Chalmerston, although not too strenuously. He knew that it didn't do to upset his wife.

'I know we do,' agreed Lady Chalmerston, and then her smile came back, but this time chilling Lord Chalmerston even more than her snarl, 'but not until we've had some fun with them first!'

Chapter Twelve

After her ordeal of the previous twenty four hours the sight of the large comfortable four-poster bed in the room that Matlock showed her to was too much for BB to resist. No sooner was the door shut than she threw herself down on it and fell fast asleep.

Ben, however, was more cautious. He was a veteran of life on the streets where his survival depended on being on his guard. Once Matlock had shown Ben to his room, the boy immediately began checking the whole room for secret panels or traps. Only after an exhaustive search of the wooden-panelled walls had revealed nothing out of the ordinary did Ben settle down to sleep, and even then he only cat-napped, ever on the alert for a footstep or any other movement in the room.

BB woke up in the middle of the afternoon, feeling refreshed and invigorated.

Remembering Lady Chalmerston's words she opened up the wardrobe in the room, and then stepped back in delight and astonishment. There before her was an array of dresses the like of which she'd never seen outside a fancy dress party. Red, green, blue, white, ornamented, plain, and all in pure silk. She was still examining them in wonder when there was a tap at her door, and then Ben slipped in.

'Ready?' he whispered.

'Not yet,' said BB. 'Frankly it's going to take me hours to decide which dress to wear.'

'I'm talking about escaping out of here,' said Ben, still talking in low tones.

BB stared at him, bewildered.

'Escaping?' she repeated incredulously.

Ben put a finger to his lips, at the same time looking around the room.

'Sssh!! Someone might be listening!'

BB laughed.

'Don't be so ridiculous! We are guests here, and we are going to be *eating*! Genuine food! Do you think I'm going to run away from that?!'

'I dunno,' said Ben suspiciously. 'It don't smell right to me.'

'What smelled right was that food on the table. Come on, it must be dinner-time. I'm starving.'

She could tell by the doubtful expression on Ben's face that he wasn't convinced.

'Look, they are a genuine seventeenth century lord and lady,' she pointed out. 'Aristocracy. Why should they harm us?'

'He was gonna have us shot!' Ben pointed out.

'Don't be silly, that was when he thought we were Roundhead spies.'

'So what changed his mind?' demanded Ben. 'I still don't like it.'

BB turned away from him and began sorting through the array of dresses again, choosing one to wear.

'Don't worry,' she told him. 'Trust me. After what we've been through, I think we've found a place of safety.'

* * *

94

A few hours later BB and Ben were sitting down to dine with the Chalmerstons. Ben had been persuaded to put on a blue velvet suit for the occasion, although he had objected strongly at first, pointing out that 'I feel an idiot in this!'

'If it's any consolation, you look an idiot,' BB had told him, 'but it's what people wear in this day and age, and we mustn't give them grounds for suspicion.'

'Talking about suspicion,' Ben had cautioned her before they went down to dinner, 'you'd better not go on about coming from the future again. I bet this lot burn witches as well.'

The meal was splendid and BB and Ben ate as if they hadn't eaten for days, which – including their travelling in time – they hadn't. Ben in particular took great care to sneak some of the more portable food off the table and into his pockets, all ready for when he and BB would be able to make their escape. He didn't want to get caught without provisions again.

Matlock doubled as butler, walking around the table, serving food as ordered, although with glowering looks at BB and Ben. The dinner was such a relaxing affair that BB was nearly caught out when Lady Chalmerston began the gentle social chit-chat.

'Tell me, my dear,' she said at one point, popping a grape into her mouth. 'Where are you from?'

BB grinned. 'I'm from about three hundred and sixty . . .' she caught Ben's warning look and she stopped herself just in time. 'Three hundred and sixty miles away.'

'Really?' smiled Lady Chalmerston. And then she turned to give Ben a simpering smile.

'And how old's your little boy?'

'Who?' said BB, baffled, and then she realized that

Lady Chalmerston was looking at Ben and she laughed. 'Oh, him! He's not my little boy!'

'She's my sister,' said Ben quickly.

Lord Chalmerston studied the pair of them and frowned.

'You don't look very much alike,' he commented.

'No,' said BB, 'he takes after the dog.'

A sudden bumping noise from the room above made them all look up at the ceiling.

'Big mice?' asked Ben.

Lady Chalmerston summoned Matlock over from the sideboard where he was busy slicing a large ham.

'Matlock,' she asked, 'what is that noise?'

'Quite possibly the ghost, milady,' said Matlock, stone-faced.

Lady Chalmerston nodded and smiled.

'Of course!' she exclaimed delightedly.

BB looked at her in awe.

'You've got a ghost?!' she said.

Lady Chalmerston nodded.

'One of Roddy's ancestors,' she explained. 'He murdered twenty-seven people in one night, here in this very house. He chopped them up with an axe and then served them to his guests for dinner.'

At this story Ben looked down at the meat on his plate suspiciously. He'd been trying to work out what it was all evening.

'It's said that he still walks at night,' added Lord Chalmerston.

There was an enormous crash from the room above, and once again they all looked up.

'It sounds like he also falls over,' commented Ben.

BB shook her head. This was wonderful! Not only

96

was she actually eating in a genuine seventeenth century manor house, but it had a real live ghost!

The rest of the meal passed without incident. After it was over Lord and Lady Chalmerston said that they hoped their guests would excuse them, but after such a tiring day they were sure they would understand. BB responded with equal courtesy, thanking the Chalmerstons for such exquisite hospitality, and then all four made their way to their bedrooms.

Ben didn't sleep. It wasn't only the fact that he'd rested in the daytime, it was this feeling that he had that all was not well in this place. He didn't like Lord and Lady Chalmerston. Despite their good manners there was something nasty about them just under the surface.

As he lay on his bed he heard voices murmuring beneath his window, and he went to his window and looked out. Below in the courtyard Matlock, his rifle tucked under his arm, was talking to a servant who was holding one of the fierce dogs on a leash. Didn't Matlock ever sleep? thought Ben.

Ben strained to hear what Matlock was saying, but it was nothing sinister, just instructions to the servant to keep his eyes peeled, although he made Ben's skin creep when he added: 'If you see anyone creeping around, set the dogs on them. It'll save feeding them.'

It was when he was at the window that Ben thought he heard a noise downstairs, the sound of chains rattling, and his heart stopped momentarily, and then began beating much faster. Surely it couldn't be the ghost?

Cautiously, careful not to make any noise, he crept to his door, opened it, and crept out into the passageway.

* * *

Downstairs in the banqueting room Lady Chalmerston was busy applying white paint to Lord Chalmerston's face. Lord Chalmerston sat looking pretty unhappy about the whole business, dressed in an old battered suit of armour. Nearby, leaning against the sideboard, was a large battle axe with a very sharp double blade.

'What I want to know is why is it always me who has to be the ghost?' demanded Lord Chalmerston petulantly.

'Because you're the only one who can fit in the suit of armour,' his wife replied.

'Well I don't see . . .'

Whatever it was he was going to say was smothered as she poked the paintbrush into his mouth, causing him to cough and splutter and spit out white paint.

'Do you have to open your mouth while I'm painting?' Lady Chalmerston complained.

'I was about to say that I don't see why we have to keep murdering people.'

Lady Chalmerston bent down so that she was staring him directly in the face.

'I thought you enjoyed out little hobby. You're not getting *boring*, are you, Roddy?' she hissed, and not for the first time Lord Chalmerston shuddered.

'No of course not, my petal,' he blustered. 'It's just . . .'

'Because you know what I do to *boring* people?' said Lady Chalmerston.

Lord Chalmerston gulped and decided it was safer to drop the subject. He knew only too well. There were already at least seven bodies buried in the cellar of the Manor. Not to mention those that had gone to feed the dogs.

Lady Chalmerston put the finishing touches to his nose and chin, then stepped back and admired her handiwork.

'You make a wonderful ghost,' she smiled. 'Simply terrifying. Up you get.'

Lord Chalmerston got to his feet with a great deal of clanking from the armour and a rattling of the chains that hung down from the breastplate.

'With a bit of luck when she sees you she'll simply die of fright, like the last two,' said Lady Chalmerston chattily. 'But if she doesn't . . .'

And she went over to the axe and ran her thumb along the edge of the blade meaningfully. Lord Chalmerston gulped. The haunting was all very well, but the killing. . . ! He shivered.

Lady Chalmerston smiled.

'Come on,' she said. 'Up you go. We'll just kill the woman tonight, we'll keep the boy for tomorrow. And don't make any mistakes. I'll be watching you from behind the mirror.'

Chapter Thirteen

The mirror that Lady Chalmerston referred to was the tall mirror set in the wood panelling of BB's room, the same one in which BB had admired herself while selecting the dress she had chosen to wear at dinner. Behind it was a secret passage which connected with the Chalmerston's bedroom, and in the glass was a tiny flaw through which Lady Chalmerston, safely ensconced in the secret passage, now peered into BB's room.

The door of BB's room creaked open and the figure of Lord Chalmerston clanked in, the axe held tightly in his hands, chains rattling against the battered armour.

He peered at the bed and saw the figure of BB, lying fast asleep in the bed, the covers pulled up and almost covering her. Despite his entrance, she didn't stir.

That's the trouble with letting the guests eat too much, thought Lady Chalmerston, it makes them sleep too soundly.

Lord Chalmerston approached the sleeping figure and let out a moan. He knew that his wife would be watching, and he knew that she liked to see the fear on the faces of their victims. But BB still didn't move.

He jerked about a bit, causing the chains to rattle some more, but obviously this young woman was a very sound sleeper. He groaned, not for effect but because he knew that if she didn't wake, it would mean that he would have to use the axe on her, and he hated using the axe. He also hated smothering people with pillows, and strangling them, but if he didn't he knew *he* would be the one being smothered, or strangled. And before that happened he would suffer terribly at his wife's hands.

He gave another groan and moved a step nearer the bed, the suit of armour clanking as he did so.

Behind the mirror Lady Chalmerston urged her husband to hurry up. Go on! she whispered to herself. Axe her!

Lord Chalmerston was now at the bed, and the woman still hadn't moved. He sighed. Oh well, if she wouldn't wake up to be frightened to death, then he was left with no alternative. Closing his eyes he raised the axe above his head, and then brought it down on the sleeping figure.

There was a terrible chonk! as the axe-head embedded itself deep in the figure in the bed. Then, in the moonlight, Lord Chalmerston saw dark liquid seeping out from the blankets where the axe had struck. Blood!

He shivered and tugged the axe out and then hurried to the door, the armour clanking and the chains rattling. Behind the mirror, Lady Chalmerston smiled delightedly to herself. Another one to help feed the dogs, she thought, and she hurried along the secret passage back to their bedroom to help her husband take off the armour.

Inside the room a full minute passed, then BB and Ben rolled out from under the large four-poster bed.

BB was the first to her feet. She pulled back the bedclothes to reveal the pillows and the long bolster, made up to look like a sleeping person, now split open with feathers strewn around, the whole soaked with beetroot from beetroots that Ben had stolen from the table at dinner.

BB stared down at the mess in horror.

'They tried to kill me!' she said, horrified.

'I told ya something was rotten here,' said Ben.

But BB was already striding across to the dressing table, opening it up and taking out her clothes.

'What are you doing?' asked Ben.

'I'm leaving,' said BB. 'Turn around, I'm going to dress.'

Ben shook his head.

'You can't,' he said. 'I overheard that Matlock bloke giving the servants orders. They've got guards posted all around the building outside with orders to shoot on sight.'

'They won't shoot us. We're guests.'

'No? They just tried to chop you up,' Ben pointed out.

BB stopped her dressing as she mulled over Ben's words.

'You're right,' she said thoughtfully. 'We'll sneak past them.'

'We can't,' said Ben. 'They've also got the dogs.'

'Dogs?' said BB.

'And they look hungry, remember?' said Ben.

BB moved away from the dressing table, banging her fists together in fury.

'How could they!' she raged, but in a lowered voice so as not to bring the Chalmerstons back. 'I trusted them! Ooh, I'd like to teach them a lesson!'

Ben grinned because a thought had just occurred to him. It had been a long time since he'd played a good joke on anyone, and if anyone deserved a joke played on them it was the Chalmerstons.

'We can if you want,' he said syly.

'What do you mean?' asked BB.

'Well, they think you're dead,' grinned Ben. 'Why don't we dress *you* up as a ghost. Give them a fright. Who knows, in all the confusion we might even be able to get away tonight.'

BB nodded. After what the Chalmerstons had tried to do to her tonight they deserved to be frightened. No, not just frightened, terrified out of their lives!

'I like it,' she said. 'What a pity we don't have anything from my laboratory, we could do it brilliantly.'

Ben shifted awkwardly.

'We might have one or two small things,' he said.

Then, as BB watched, Ben dipped into his pockets, and out came a roll of nylon cord, a small torch, a screwdriver, and a few other small items that had obviously come from her laboratory. She looked at them, her mouth open, then she turned to Ben.

'You are a despicable low-down thief,' she said. Before Ben could protest, she added: 'Luckily for us. Right, let's see what we've got and what we can do with them.'

It took BB just a few minutes, after sorting through the bits and pieces that Ben had 'borrowed' and examining the curtain rods and the furniture in the room, to decide how she could best use them.

'I'm going to rig up a pulley system,' she announced. 'Do you know how a pulley system works?'

'No,' said Ben.

'The idea is that gears of different ratios give a differential that means a large load can be hauled up by a small body.'

Ben frowned.

'I'm a small body,' he said.

'You've got it,' said BB. 'Let's get going.'

* * *

In the Chalmerston's bedroom Lord and Lady Chalmerston were fast asleep in their enormous four-poster bed. Or, rather, Lady Chalmerston was asleep; for Lord Chalmerston sleep was impossible. Every time he closed his eyes he saw the axe biting into the figure of BB, huddled beneath the blankets, and blood spurting out.

Beside him, his wife snored, oblivious to any fears or nightmares. He shook her, gently.

'Are you awake, my petal?' he asked querulously.

'No,' growled back Lady Chalmerston.

Lord Chalmerston gulped, then continued: 'Sometimes I think the ghosts of the people we've murdered are watching us. Don't you?'

His only answer was a loud snore from his deeply sleeping wife. He sighed and slipped down beneath the bedclothes, closing his eyes, determined to try to get some sleep.

That was when he heard it: a voice somewhere out in the house, a woman's voice, ghostly, moaning. He sat up in bed, wide awake at once.

'Who . . . who . . . who's there?' he quavered.

The moaning ceased. Shivering, he shook his wife, but she growled sleepily at him: 'Go to sleep.' And she gave another loud snore.

Outside the room, from somewhere in the house, Lord Chalmerston heard the voice again, this time calling faintly to him: 'Lord Chalmerston . . .'

His first instinct was to hide himself completely under the blankets, but there was something hypnotic about the voice. Shaking all over, he slid out of bed, picked up a candle in a candle-holder, lit it, and walked with trembling steps towards the door.

At the very top of the ornate staircase, four floors

up, Ben was in charge of the pulley system which BB
had rigged up: a cloth was wrapped round his hand as
he pulled on the nylon twine. Suspended from the nylon
twine, BB swung in the stairwell. She was wearing the
same dress she had worn at dinner and now, using make-
up she had found in one of the drawers, her face was
painted a deathly white, her eyes hollowed out with
black eye-paint. Scarlet rouge made the mark of an axe
blow across her face. Fixed to her necklace was the
small torch, aimed upwards so that the effect on her face
was one of nightmarish horror.

'Lord Chalmerston . . .' she groaned softly again, her
voice echoing eerily through the still house, and then she
saw Chalmerston, creeping along the passage, candle
held aloft, his whole body shaking with fear.

'Hello?' he called in a nervous whisper.

BB picked up the hem of the dress and flapped it and
the gust of wind blew out Chalmerston's candle. She saw
him jump in alarm, and at the same time he turned, and
saw BB.

Chalmerston clutched at his heart as he saw the
white-faced ghost of the woman he had just killed hanging in mid-air, looking directly at him with eyes that
glinted in hollow sockets.

'Aargh!' he screamed, and then he stumbled
forward, missed his footing, and crashed and tumbled
all the way down the stairs to the very bottom,
ending up with a smash against an ornamental suit of
armour.

'Get me up!' whispered BB hoarsely to Ben.
Straightaway he began to haul on the nylon twine and
BB sailed upwards. They were just in time because the
sound of Lord Chalmerston crashing down the stairs so
noisily had brought Lady Chalmerston violently out of

her sleep, and she now stumbled angrily out of the bedroom.

'What on earth is all that row?!' she bellowed.

The noise of metallic clanking and groaning brought her attention to the bottom of the stairs. She looked over the banisters and saw Lord Chalmerston lying in the chaos of a dismembered suit of armour, clutching his head and groaning.

'You idiot!' she raged, and she stomped down the stairs towards her unfortunate husband.

At the top of the stairs Ben was suddenly having trouble with the pulley. He didn't know whether BB hadn't made it properly, or whether he wasn't working it correctly, but suddenly there was a dull crack! and a piece of wood fell off. The result, for BB, was terrifying. One second she was going up, the next she was hurtling down the stairwell at a terrifying speed.

She was just about to open her mouth to scream, when the nylon jerked taut and she stopped abruptly and found herself dangling just two metres from the floor at the bottom of the stairs, like a puppet on a string.

She held her breath, desperate not to make a sound, because only a short distance away Lady Chalmerston had now arrived at her fallen husband and was helping him to his feet, while tearing him off a strip for sleepwalking and waking her. Lord Chalmerston protested volubly.

'I saw her! I saw her ghost!'

'Stuff and nonsense! There are no such things as ghosts!' snorted Lady Chalmerston.

And she turned to wave her arms at the house to back up her statement, and that was when she saw BB dangling apparently in mid-air.

109

Her scream echoed through the house. In fact it was so loud it possibly went through the whole county. It was certainly loud enough to bring Matlock and two other servants running, all armed with muskets.

'I'm here my lady!' said Matlock.

Lady Chalmerston pointed at the suspended BB.

'Shoot it!' she urged. 'Shoot the ghost!'

Matlock hesitated only a second while the thought ran through his head: how can you shoot a ghost? Then he put his musket to his shoulder and aimed at BB's head.

Luckily for BB, at that moment at the top of the stairs the nylon string and the pulley finally disintegrated. The result was that BB crashed to the floor, just as Matlock pulled the trigger, and his bullet crashed into the wall instead of her head.

In that instant Matlock and Lady Chalmerston realized what was going on. Urgently Matlock gestured to the two other servants to hurry up the stairs.

'Bring down the boy!' he ordered.

The two servants ran up the stairs as commanded, rifles at the ready, while Lady Chalmerston went to the fallen BB.

'Oh well done, my dear!' she said, and her smile did indeed look genuine. 'How nice to have a worthy opponent for our little games.'

'Games?' said BB, struggling to her feet, still tangled up with the twine. 'You call killing people "games"?'

'You want me to shoot her again, my lady?' asked Matlock, who had now reloaded his rifle.

Lady Chalmerston shook her head.

'No, nothing so crude,' she said. 'It's been a long time since we've had someone who joined in the spirit of things. What do you think we should do with them, Roddy?'

Her husband was still fuming over the terror he had felt when he had seen the apparition of BB floating in the stairwell, and the aches and bumps he had experienced during his fall down the stairs.

'I think she ought to be boiled in oil!' he snorted.

'Yes, you would,' said Lady Chalmerston, not impressed. She smiled at BB. 'No imagination, my husband.'

The two servants appeared down the stairs, dragging Ben with them.

BB glared at Ben.

'It was the thing you made that broke!' said Ben defensively.

'It was the way you worked it!' said BB.

'Now now. You'll have plenty of time to argue over whose fault it was,' Lady Chalmerston chided them. 'Matlock?'

'Yes, milady?'

'I want them under very secure guard tonight. If they escape, I shall kill you.'

'Yes, milady.'

Lord Chalmerston was still thinking up terrible ways for BB and Ben to die.

'Stretched on a rack and *then* boiled in oil,' he snarled through gritted teeth.

'How boring,' said Lady Chalmerston dismissively. 'No, I've got something much more exciting in mind. At dawn tomorrow we shall all go hunting.'

Ben frowned, puzzled. Hunting? That didn't sound much like a punishment. For her part, BB shook her head firmly.

'I'm sorry but I'm totally against hunting,' she told

111

them. 'I believe that every animal has a right to live and die in a civilized manner.'

Lady Chalmerston smiled her wolfish smile.

'Then you'll just love this hunt, my dear,' she cooed. 'No animals.'

BB looked at her, surprised.

'No animals?' she said.

And suddenly BB and Ben realized what Lady Chalmerston meant. *They* were to be the quarry! They were to be hunted by those savage dogs!

Chapter Fourteen

BB and Ben spent an uncomfortable night chained to a wooden post in a stable. On either side of them servants sat and watched, rifles on the alert, and outside in the night dogs sniffed and growled, and Matlock patrolled the grounds, rifle always at the ready. There was no chance of escape.

As dawn rose BB and Ben were dragged into the courtyard of the Manor. They saw that the hunt had already been assembled: Lord and Lady Chalmerston and various other people on horseback, and servants milling around holding the fierce snarling dogs on leashes.

Lord Chalmerston waited until BB and Ben had been dragged into the centre of the courtyard, then he cleared his throat and addressed the hunting party.

'The other day,' he announced, 'we discovered these two Roundhead spies near our property. Obviously trying to kill us all.'

At this there were growls from the servants and sneers from the mounted riders.

'Now wait just a minute. . . !' began BB.

'Shoot them if they talk, Matlock,' smiled Lady Chalmerston. 'It's so rude to interrupt.'

'Yes, milady,' nodded Matlock, and aimed his rifle at BB.

'Because my wife and I are merciful people,' continued Lord Chalmerston, 'we've decided to give them a sporting chance. To run for their lives.' He took out a large fob watch and peered closely at it. 'We shall give you two minutes start. I think that's a sporting chance. Beginning now. Let the dogs have the scent.'

The servants let the dogs pad close to BB and Ben, the animals' slavering jaws pushing into their clothes as they sniffed and snuffled.

'You can't hunt us with dogs!' shouted BB. 'It's cruel! I refuse to take part in this . . . this barbaric practice.'

'You have one minute fifty seconds,' said Chalmerston, looking at his watch, and he began to count down: 'One minute forty nine.'

'Come on,' said Ben, and he tugged at BB's arm. 'They're going to do it anyway.'

BB hesitated, then as she looked at Lord and Lady Chalmerston smiling at each other, a feeling of anger surged through her. I won't give them the satisfaction of dying this easily! she said determinedly to herself. And she and Ben ran out of the courtyard, the dogs barking and growling after them, straining at the leashes.

* * *

BB and Ben ran, the breath rasping in their throats, the hard-baked uneven earth making running difficult. Behind them they could hear the baying of the hounds, and behind the hounds the thunder of horses' hooves and the wail of hunting horns.

Luckily for them the countryside was wooded so they were able to run through the cover of trees, which, although it gave them sight cover from the hunters, did not give them cover from the dogs.

'A stream!' shouted BB, and she ran to the stream

and splashed into its shallows, Ben following. 'With a bit of luck the water might throw the dogs off the scent!'

And they began to run upstream, water splashing up, the pain in BB's chest getting worse with each step as she drove herself on. Suddenly she sank down in the water.

'Come on!' urged Ben. 'They're not far behind.'

'I can't run any further!' gasped BB. 'I never have been able to do this. I hated cross-country when I was at school.'

Ben looked desperately around them as the baying of the dogs came nearer. To one side of the stream was a small clump of trees, and Ben pointed at them.

'Quick, let's get up one of those trees!'

'What good will that do?' BB gasped.

'Dogs can't climb trees.'

Ben grabbed BB and hauled her to her feet and hurried, half-supporting her, to the clump of trees.

'Up you go,' he said, and BB reached up, grabbed the lower branch, and began to haul herself painfully up into the cover of the branches of the tree.

Lord and Lady Chalmerston and the other riders cantered on their horses, secure in the knowledge that, on foot, the fugitives had no chance. The dogs were already at the shallow stream, sniffing and barking at the water's edge, and then barking and yelping and growling, before following the scent. A short distance later the pursuing dogs reached the point where BB and Ben had left the stream and ran for the clump of trees, and they ran after the scent, barking excitedly.

The hunters caught up with the dogs a few minutes later and found them jumping up at the tree which was BB and Ben's hiding place.

The hunters exchanged satisfied smiles and

115

dismounted, Lord Chalmerston was the first at the foot of the tree. He pushed the dogs aside, looked up at the thick cover of leaves, and called up: 'Caught you! Come on down!'

In the cover of the leaves BB and Ben looked at each other, trapped, but still defiant.

'I'm not giving them that pleasure!' snapped BB to Ben, and she called down the tree to Chalmerston and the other hunters: 'We're not coming down to be torn apart by dogs!'

'Of course not!' came Lady Chalmerston's voice, containing more than a note of indignation as it floated back up the tree. 'How can you think that we'd do such an uncivilized thing!'

BB and Ben exchanged puzzled glances. If that was the case then what had this hunt been about?

'What do you think?' BB asked Ben.

'I think they're lying,' said Ben. 'Altogether not to be trusted.'

BB thought about it. It was certainly strange. She called back down to the hunters: 'You wouldn't?'

'Of course not!' called up Lord Chalmerston. 'You have the word of an English Lord!' Then he caught his wife's glare, and added hastily: 'And Lady.'

Up in the tree BB and Ben were in intense discussion at this sudden strange development.

'They say they're not going to have us torn apart by dogs,' said BB. 'They've even given us their word.'

Ben snorted scornfully. Their word, indeed! Then he frowned. But if they weren't going to have them torn apart, what were they going to do with them? The realization hit Ben suddenly.

'They're going to hang us as spies!' he said.

BB thought this over. It was certainly a possibility.

117

'I'll check,' she said, and she called down the tree: 'Are you going to hang us?'

At the base of the tree the hunters were getting tired of all this talking. This was supposed to be a hunt, not a philosophical debate.

'No! We are not going to hang you either!' shouted Lady Chalmerston, her patience wearing thin. 'Now come down!'

BB looked at Ben, thinking the situation over.

'They say they're not going to hang us,' she said.

'Well I don't believe them,' said Ben.

'Neither do I,' agreed BB. Her mind made up, she called down the tree: 'We don't believe you and we're not coming!'

At the base of the tree the hunters exchanged looks of restlessness. Lady Chalmerston fumed silently, then she turned and snapped: 'Matlock!'

'Yes, milady,' nodded Matlock, understanding her meaning, and he raised his rifle to his shoulder, pointed it up in the tree at the hidden BB and Ben, and fired.

* * *

BB and Ben, their hands tied in front of them, trudged along the path towards Chalmerston Manor. Behind them Matlock prodded them with the barrel of his rifle if they slowed. Behind Matlock came the hunt. Lord and Lady Chalmerston led on horseback, and behind the mounted riders came the servants with the dogs, plus other servants carrying an assortment of rifles and muskets. Matlock's shot up into the trees had been enough to convince BB and Ben that unless they came down they would be shot there and then, and so they had

118

clambered down the tree and then been tied up and force-marched back towards the manor.

As the party neared the red brick walls that surrounded the courtyard of the manor house, Lord Chalmerston's voice rang out 'Stop!', and the procession halted.

'Place the prisoners against the wall,' ordered Chalmerston.

BB and Ben exchanged worried looks as they were grabbed by servants and hustled over to the wall surrounding the Manor. What was going on?

'You promised you wouldn't kill us!' called BB.

'No,' smiled Lady Chalmerston. 'We said we wouldn't have you torn apart by dogs or hanged. That's why you're going to be shot.'

At this the Chalmerstons, the other hunters and the servants laughed out loud, enjoying Lady Chalmerston's joke hugely. Even Matlock managed a small smile as he pushed BB and Ben against the wall. He pulled two lengths of grimy rag from his pocket, and proceeded to tie them around BB's and Ben's eyes as makeshift blindfolds.

That done he withdrew to order the servants with the muskets and rifles into a semblance of a line to act as a firing squad.

While this was going on BB and Ben stood, their backs against the wall, listening to the noises and Matlock's shouted orders.

'BB?' gulped Ben tentatively.

'Yes?'

'If we get out of this, will you take me back with you?'

If the situation hadn't been so serious, BB might have been tempted to laugh.

'Where to?' she asked.

'To your time,' said Ben. 'I don't like mine much.'

'To be honest,' said BB sadly, 'I don't think we're going to get out of this.'

'No, nor do I,' said Ben, 'but if we did. Would you?'

BB hesitated. What could she say? At this time it was all pointless. Even though she knew Ben was blindfolded as she was, she turned towards the sound of his voice and smiled at him: 'Yes,' she said.

She heard the smile in Ben's voice as he said back: 'Great. I've never had anyone who wanted to look after me before.'

Then they both heard Matlock call out: 'Squad, positions!'

There was the sound of muskets being made ready, the clicking of metal against metal.

'Take aim!' called Matlock.

There was what seemed the shortest of all possible pauses, then Matlock barked out: 'Fire!', and there was the explosion of many rifles and muskets being fired simultaneously. . . .

Chapter Fifteen

The sound of the musket volley echoed around the open countryside. Their backs pressed against the brick wall, their bodies and minds tensed against the hail of bullets, BB and Ben closed their eyes behind their blindfolds and held their breath . . . and nothing happened.

Slowly, hesitantly, BB and Ben touched their bound hands against their chests, then the rest of their bodies. Nothing. No bullet holes, no marks. Was this what being dead was like?

Ben was the first to reach up to his blindfold and pull it down, BB doing the same thing a second later.

An amazing sight met their eyes. In front of them lay the firing squad, and Matlock, and Lord and Lady Chalmerston, and the rest of the hunters, all sprawled out in positions of death on the ground, their bodies riddled with bullets.

Ben turned to BB, his mouth hanging open in amazement. He knew this woman could do incredible things, but this was beyond belief! 'How did you do that?!' he exclaimed.

BB shook her head, equally stunned.

'Nothing to do with me!' she said.

A noise to one side made them look round, and then they saw, appearing from around the corner of the manor wall, a party of Roundhead soldiers, all carrying rifles with smoke coming from the barrels. At the head of the party was the familiar figure of the captain of the

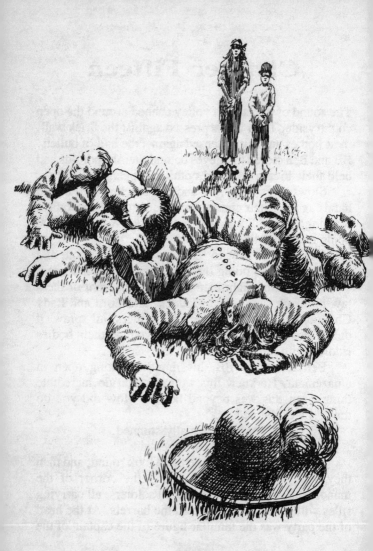

guard, and he approached BB and Ben, a smile on his face.

'Good!' he said. 'I hate to lose prisoners!'

* * *

As BB and Ben marched under guard into the courtyard of the castle, BB reflected that they seemed to be doing an awful lot of walking around tied up. It was obviously an occupational hazard of living during the English Civil War.

BB noticed that, during their short absence, the camp in the courtyard had grown in size. No longer did it just consist of tents and soldiers. Now market stalls had sprung up selling food, offering haircuts and livestock. Despite their situation BB nudged Ben.

'Isn't this fantastic!' she said, her voice full of awe. 'Notice how this place has gone from just a military camp to a small town in just two days! Don't you find it incredible!'

Ben glared back at her. Honestly, this woman was such an idiot! Here they were, threatened with death for the umpteenth time, and all she could think of was how great this place looked.

'No,' he snapped back. 'They're gonna kill us!'

'Don't be silly,' said BB. 'If they were going to do that they'd have let the Royalists shoot us. They've brought us back here for a purpose.'

'Yeah, to burn you as a witch,' Ben pointed out.

'Silence!' roared the captain, and the procession carried on through the passageway to the inner courtyard, the only sound the thud of boots and the clanking of the soldiers' armour.

As they walked across the inner courtyard, BB

123

noticed soldiers placing bundles of straw around a wooden stake set in the middle of the courtyard, and a shudder went through her. That couldn't be for her, surely? They couldn't *really* be going to burn her!

The huge figure of Leather Hardbones was waiting for them on the steps of the castle building, and his face split into a broad and ugly smile as the procession pulled to a halt before him.

'Come back, have you, witch?' he leered at BB. 'Good. The Witchfinder General has arrived and he'd've been pretty annoyed if his journey had been wasted.' Turning to the captain he ordered: 'Take charge here while I take 'em to the church to meet Master Hopkins.'

* * *

Hardbones, accompanied by two armed soldiers, escorted BB and Ben along a path at the back of the castle, round the huge stone buildings, to a stone church set back from the castle.

When Hardbones pushed open the heavy wooden door and ushered BB and Ben in, they both stopped in surprise at the scene that presented itself to them:

At the front of the church in front of the altar stood BB's Yamaha with the two crash helmets placed on top of the seat.

Kneeling in front of the motorcycle, his hands clasped together as if in prayer and his face lifted towards the stained glass of the church window as if seeking comfort, was the crouching figure of Matthew Hopkins, the Witchfinder General.

As BB and Ben were pushed down the aisle towards the front of the church and they drew near Hopkins, BB found herself being surprised. After all the talk of the

124

Witchfinder General she had expected some devil in human form, some hideous being. Instead here was this kneeling man, quite small in appearance, dressed all in black gazing up at Heaven with an almost saintly smile on his face. Admittedly she could only see one side of his face, but there was no reason to doubt that the saintly smile didn't extend to the other side. A feeling of relief ran through her. Here was a reasonable man!

'He doesn't look so bad to me!' she whispered to Ben. 'I think we're going to be all right here.'

Hopkins obviously became aware of their presence, because he came out of his reverie and turned towards them, rising from his knees as he did so. As he rose and they saw him full face both BB and Ben gave little gasps of horror. The smile that BB had seen had only been on one side of his face, the other side was hideously scarred and it was this scarring that pulled his mouth into the smile. Now that smile was mocking, terrifying.

Now that he stood up they also saw that he was not small, that that had been an illusion created by Hopkins kneeling with his legs cramped under him. Now as he approached them he towered above them, a thin terrifying angular figure, his black cape hanging down making him look like an avenging angel of evil.

'You were saying?' Ben whispered back with a gulp.

'I've brought the witches, Master Hopkins, as I promised,' said Hardbones, and they could tell by the tremor in the Roundhead commander's voice the awe and fear in which he also held the Witchfinder.

Hopkins stood looking BB and Ben full in the face, his eyes in that horrific scarred face taking them in. When at last he spoke it was in a voice that was gentle, but its very gentleness sent shivers of fear through everyone in the church.

'So,' he said, quietly but intensely, 'you are witches.'

Nervously both BB and Ben shook their heads from side to side in denial of this statement. Hopkins moved to BB and held his open hand in front of her mouth.

'Breathe,' he commanded her softly.

'Cold hands, eh?' said BB, her voice quivering with nervousness. 'Bad circulation. My Uncle Peter suffers from that.'

'Breathe,' commanded Hopkins, his order firmer this time.

BB breathed out. Hopkins closed his hand, catching BB's breath in his palm. Then he took it to his nose, opened his palm, and inhaled. BB and Ben watched this process nervously. Hopkins seemed to ponder something in his mind, then he turned to BB and nodded. When he spoke his voice was the same gentle voice as before, but the words were terrifying: 'The witch smell. You have it.'

'It's garlic,' said BB quickly. 'We had a very rich meal last night with some Royalists . . .'

'Silence!' barked Hopkins, and BB's voice shuddered to a stop. When Hopkins spoke again, however, it was in the same sad and gentle tone as before, as if he was himself suffering deep torment as a result of BB's situation.

'When did you first make your pact with Satan?' he asked.

BB gulped. She knew she had to make this man see reason.

'Please, Mr Hopkins, you're an intelligent man,' she began. 'I'm sure you don't really believe this stuff about witches . . .'

Hopkins shook his head sadly and slowly, reached out and took her hands in his, caressingly.

'Do not fear,' he said gently. 'Together we will save your soul.'

'Shall I heat up some irons, Master Hopkins?' asked Leather Hardbones, wanting to be seen to be helpful by this powerful man.

Hopkins shook his head and released BB's hands.

'That will not be necessary,' he said. Turning to BB he added: 'Will it? Your heart cries out to confess.'

BB forced a smile. She was in terrible danger, but she had to try to get through to this man who held her life in the balance.

'Honestly, I've got nothing to confess. I'm not a witch.'

'Then who are you? And where are you from?' asked Hopkins.

Great! thought BB miserably. Why do people always start with the hard ones first?

Hopkins had now moved away from BB and had gone to Ben. The Witchfinder bent down and sniffed Ben's hair.

'That's just dirt,' BB commented, trying to be helpful. 'Though I'd watch out for head lice and nits.'

Hopkins turned away from Ben with a dismissive gesture.

'The boy is just a familiar. Place him in the stocks, we may have use for him later.'

'I am afraid there isn't room in the stocks for the boy at the moment, Master Hopkins,' grovelled Hardbones apologetically. 'I have been so successful at capturing prisoners . . .'

Hopkins held up his hand to stop the Roundhead commander.

'Then make room,' he said. 'Remove one of the wretches who at present inhabits them. There must be someone who is due for freedom . . . or for death?'

Hardbones gulped and nodded, his nod almost becoming a bow.

'Right, Master Hopkins.'

'As for the witch,' said Hopkins, turning once more to BB, 'lock her away until she is ready to burn.'

Burn! The word went through BB and filled her with terror. As the two soldiers grabbed her and began to drag her towards the door of the church she burst out:

'I am not a witch! Mr Hopkins, please! I have to tell you the truth!'

Hopkins stopped as he was about to turn back to the motorcycle and held up his hand for the soldiers to wait.

'I am listening,' he said, his eyes watching her carefully.

BB gulped. All right, Ben had warned her about talking about coming from the future, but she was going to burn as a witch anyway. She had nothing to lose, she had to try it!

'What I'm going to tell you may sound unbelievable,' she said. 'Possibly even shocking.'

Hopkins's face didn't alter, his scarred face still watching her intently.

'Nothing that you have to say can shock me,' he said, his voice as gentle as before.

'And you'll listen?'

Hopkins nodded gravely.

'Of course.'

BB took a deep breath, and then began:

'Mr Hopkins, the truth is I have come from three hundred and sixty years in the future.' She pointed to the motorbike standing in front of the altar. 'On that. With

129

him.' And here she gestured towards Ben. 'This is not witchery, it's science.' When Hopkins didn't say anything, just looked at her impassively, she continued, warming to her theme. 'Can't you see it's an incredible thing to be speaking to people from three hundred and sixty years in the future? Don't you want to *know* what will happen in three hundred and sixty years?!' She looked at Hopkins, then at the bewildered Hardbones, then back at Hopkins again, her voice catching fire with the excitement that she felt at being able to talk about this at last: 'People will have landed on the moon! In the future we can see people all over the world by satellites!' she grinned ruefully. 'The trains still won't run on time, of course. Though you haven't got trains yet. Don't you think this is wonderful!'

There was a silence in the church while Hopkins seemed to weigh all that BB had said, then he forced what BB hoped looked like a smile. When he spoke his voice was sad, sorrowful.

'Your possession by the devil is worse than I feared,' he said sadly. To Hardbones he said: 'Lock them away. I will attend the witch before we burn her.'

And he watched as Hardbones and the two soldiers dragged BB and Ben back down the aisle to the church door.

'I am not a witch!' screamed BB desperately. 'I'm not!'

But Hopkins had turned away from them, and even now was taking his place kneeling at the altar to examine this devilish device that the witch had brought with her.

Chapter Sixteen

The door of the cell clanged shut and Hardbones turned the key in the lock, grinned at BB and Ben through the bars, and went off along the passage, the heels of his boots ringing on the wet flagstones of the underground passage.

BB and Ben were back in the same cell they had occupied previously, only now they were the only occupants.

BB stood at the cell door, holding on to the bars, her shoulders slumped as she watched Hardbones swagger the length of the passage and disappear around the corner. As soon as the Roundhead commander had gone, BB's posture changed and she whirled on Ben, her expression urgent.

'Right, where's the key?'

Ben looked at her blankly.

'What key?' he asked.

'The last time this happened you stole the key to the door from the guard. Remember?'

'That was *last* time,' said Ben. 'They'd be watching out for it this time. You gotta be like lightning, you can't strike in the same place twice.'

'I don't want a weather report, I want a key to get us out of here!' snapped BB, annoyed.

'Well I ain't got one,' shrugged Ben.

BB stared at him, then her shoulders slumped and

she dropped her head and moaned: 'Oh God, I'm going to die!'

'No you're not. . . ,' said Ben, going to her, trying to be comforting.

'Yes I am!' insisted BB.

Ben thought it over.

'Yeah,' I suppose you are,' he admitted ruefully.

BB glared at him, furious.

'You're a fat lot of use! What sort of thing is that to say?'

'You said it first!' Ben pointed out.

BB paced the cell, wringing her hands as she thought about her fate.

'It's all right for you,' she moaned. 'You're just going to be stuck in the stocks and have things thrown at you.'

Things thrown at him? Ben frowned, he didn't like the sound of this.

'What sort of things?' he asked.

'Food,' said BB. 'Rocks. . . .'

'Rocks?!' echoed the horrified Ben. 'I'll be killed!'

'We've got to get out of here!' said BB with a fierce determination. 'I will not be burned as a witch! For a start, don't these people know how ecologically unsound burning all that straw is? Don't they know the problems the Greenhouse Effect is causing this planet?'

'Maybe we could start a fire in the cell?' suggested Ben thoughtfully.

'What, and burn to death quicker?' demanded BB.

'No, then they'd open the doors to let us out and we could escape!'

Before he could develop this idea any further there was the sound of footsteps approaching. There was the sound of the key turning in the lock, then the cell door

132

swung open and the captain of the guard and two soldiers appeared at the cell door.

'Right, we've got a place in the stocks for you,' snapped the captain. 'Take him out.'

Before the soldiers could grab hold of him, Ben took the initiative and walked towards the open door, taking hold of BB's hand as he passed and pulling her along with him.

The soldiers and the captain exchanged puzzled looks at this.

'She's with me,' explained Ben airily.

It didn't work. The captain of the guard stopped BB and thrust her roughly back into the cell, before grabbing Ben by the shoulder and dragging him off.

'It was worth a try!' Ben called back to BB as one of the soldiers locked the cell door again.

* * *

Out in the courtyard Ben was hustled to the stocks and saw that a man was just in the process of being removed from them, his face battered and bruised, his face and clothes, and the stocks themselves, stained and splattered with the marks of fruit and crushed vegetables.

As the soldiers lifted the top half of the wooden stocks and released the prisoner, he collapsed in a heap on the ground.

'If he wants to stay in there. . . ,' offered Ben helpfully.

At a nod from the captain two soldiers grabbed Ben and forced him over the stocks, stepping over the body of the fallen man who'd previously occupied them. Although Ben struggled, the soldiers forced his head and wrists into the holes in the wooden board, and then slammed down the top board, imprisoning him.

One of the soldiers snapped the hasp at the side of the stocks shut, holding them firmly in place. Then the two soldiers picked up the fallen man and began to drag him off.

The captain looked at the imprisoned Ben and grinned. He reached down, picked up a rotten tomato, then threw it at Ben, scoring a direct hit as the tomato exploded on the boy's face. With a roar of delighted laughter at his accuracy the captain turned and strode back towards the castle building.

* * *

In the cell BB was pacing up and down nervously when she heard footsteps approaching. She looked up as she heard a key being put into the lock, and then the door swung open and Matthew Hopkins stood there, his thin angular figure framed in the doorway. Behind him stood Leather Hardbones.

'Kneel before the Witchfinder General!' roared Hardbones.

BB gestured down at her trousers.

'Do I have to? These trousers go all baggy at the knees . . .'

Hardbones was about to advance on BB and force her to the ground, but Hopkins stopped him with a wave of his hand. He spoke to BB, his voice as soft and sad as before.

'I have come here to give you a chance to confess, before the fire.'

'Actually, I've been thinking,' said BB. 'If I confess to being a witch — not that I am — will that save me from the fire?'

Hopkins shook his head.

'The whole purpose of the fire is to save the souls of witches from being damned for eternity. Salvation by fire.'

'All right, so let's say I'm not a witch — which I'm not . . .'

'I know you *are*,' countered Hopkins.

'Look, couldn't I be saved some other way than being burnt?' begged BB, now feeling desperate. 'Some other form of punishment?' She forced a joke. 'A week in Glasgow?' And she gave what she hoped was a laugh, but even to her it sounded unreal and strangled.

'You tempt me with laughter,' said Hopkins, his manner towards her stiffening.

'Let me flog her, Master Witchfinder,' intervened Hardbones indignantly.

'Please,' begged BB, 'you've got to believe me. I have come from the future, I know what's going to happen. For example, don't you want to know who wins this war!'

At this Hardbones's ears pricked up, obviously interested, but his interest vanished when he saw Hopkins clap his hands to his ears to blot out BB's voice.

'Be quiet, witch. . . !' Hopkins raged.

'Yes! Be quiet, witch!' echoed Hardbones.

But BB pressed on, desperately clutching at this last straw to get her out of this situation.

'I can tell you what happens to you, if you'll give me a chance to go back and look you up in the history books!' she said, clutching Hopkins. 'Please, everyone wants to know their future. Is it a deal?'

Angrily Hopkins tore his hands away from his ears, grabbed BB and threw her down on the floor.

'Foul temptress!' he yelled at her. 'Before this day is done you will burn!' And turning to Hardbones he pointed at the passageway. 'Come! To the church where we shall pray and examine the devilish device further!'

With that he stormed out of the cell. Hardbones hesitated. The idea of knowing his future appealed to him, but the Witchfinder General was a powerful man.

Hardbones turned on BB, slumped down on the bench.

'Burn, witch!' he shouted at her, loudly enough for Hopkins to hear.

With that he hurried out of the cell, locked the door, and then half-ran to catch up with the Witchfinder General.

Chapter Seventeen

At the stocks, Ben was suffering. A group of off-duty soldiers had decided to entertain themselves by pelting the newest prisoner. It had started off badly enough with soft fruit, then it had moved on to hard vegetables such as turnips, and now a rock had thudded into the wood of the stocks, just above Ben's head.

'No rocks! No rocks!' yelled Ben.

In answer another rock was thrown, just missing the stocks with a metal clank! At the same time the wood holding Ben's head and wrists in place jumped slightly, and Ben frowned to himself. A metal clank?

Another rock thudded into the stocks, and Ben stopped thinking about anything except avoiding being hit. His luck was in. A sergeant appeared who decided that the men's rest period had ended.

'Right, you lot!' he barked at the soldiers. 'Collect buckets and shovels from the stores. You're on privy-cleaning duty!'

The soldiers began to grumble among themselves, but moved off in the direction of the stores to collect their tools. As soon as they were gone Ben tested the wooden part of the stocks holding him in place, and sure enough it moved! A glance at the edge of the stocks told him what had happened: the rock that had almost missed the stocks had hit the metal staple holding the two halves of the stocks in place and dislodged it. He was free!

Luckily for Ben, attention was momentarily

diverted away from him because of an argument that broke out in one of the tents as two soldiers argued over ownership of some small object. As their raised voices brought other soldiers coming to see what was going on, Ben took advantage of the attention being diverted away from him. He slipped out of the stocks and ran to a nearby tent. It was a matter of a second to slip beneath the tent canvas while he took stock of his situation. He had to get BB out of the cell and to the church, and then they could escape on that machine of hers.

He looked out from under the tent at the courtyard. If he could get to the inner courtyard he might be able to find a way in to the castle building itself, and then down to the dungeon. If.

He looked around the tent. It was empty with very little in it. Obviously whoever had been staying here had just left, taking everything with them. Then he saw, at the far side of the tent, lying half-covered by straw, the hilt of a knife just protruding. OK, it wasn't a key, but he'd opened locks with a knife before. The main thing was, it was better than nothing.

Ben checked that no-one was watching, then he hurried across the tent and picked up the knife. Now to get to BB.

* * *

'He must be around somewhere! He cannot just have vanished!'

The captain of the guard was both astonished and angry. When word had first come to him that the boy had gone he could not believe it, accusing the soldier who'd come with the message of being drunk, a serious accusation indeed as strong ale was forbidden in

Cromwell's army. But sure enough, when he had gone to look for himself, the stocks had been open and empty, and the boy gone.

Instantly he'd instituted a search, but ten minutes of searching tents, probing outbuildings, even poking around in the straw piled around the stake, had given up nothing. The captain shuddered at the prospect of going to the commander with the bad news, particularly with the Witchfinder General here, but if they couldn't find the boy then he would have no alternative.

In fact Ben was already inside the castle. He had just been wondering how to get from his hiding place in the outer courtyard to the inner courtyard, when a cart had trundled slowly past laden with logs and cut brushwood for the castle kitchen. A quick run from the cover of the tent, clambering up undetected on the back of the cart, and then wriggling his way under the loose faggots of wood at the back of the cart, and Ben was able to peer out from his mobile hiding place as the cart trundled through the passageway into the inner courtyard and creaked its way towards the rear of the castle and the small door that led to the kitchen. He was in his hiding place when his escape was noticed and the hue and cry went up for him.

The cart had pulled up at the kitchen door and the carter been called to join in the search, Ben had taken the opportunity to jump down from the cart and scurry into the kitchen, which had fortunately been empty.

From there it had been a case of creeping along narrow passageways, all the time hiding in nooks and crannies and shadowy alcoves, searching out the passage that he knew would take him down to the dungeons, and to BB.

* * *

In the church, Leather Hardbones listened attentively, almost reverently, as Matthew Hopkins paced around the motorbike and pointed out various parts of this devilish machine which he had identified.

'These are obviously the devil's horns,' said Hopkins knowledgeably, pointing to the bike's handle-bars; and then, pointing to the front indicators: 'And these are its eyes.'

Hardbones tapped the exhaust carefully and nervously.

'What do you reckon this bit is, Master Hopkins?' he asked.

Hopkins frowned, he had been puzzling over that himself. He was saved from answering by the door of the church opening and the captain of the guard coming in. From his apprehensive manner it was obvious something was wrong.

'Sir. . . ,' he said tentatively as he approached Hard-bones and Hopkins.

Hardbones bridled. Just as he had been getting on familiar terms with the Witchfinder General, terms which maybe would lead to his elevation in the revolutionary army, the spell had been broken by this idiot coming in like this.

'What's the meaning of this interruption?' he demanded. 'Can't you see I'm engaged in close consultation with the Witchfinder General himself?' He turned to Hopkins and was saying: 'I'm sorry about this, sir . . .', when the captain broke in with: 'The boy is gone!'

Hardbones's mouth dropped open.

'What?! How?!'

'Sorcery,' said Hopkins firmly. 'I should have burned the boy as well. Is the witch still secured?'

'I do not know, sir,' said the captain apologetically.

'You mean you haven't looked?!' raged Hardbones, furious at the way he was being let down by this fool in the presence of the Witchfinder General. 'Idiot!'

For his part, Hopkins was already hurrying to the door of the church, murmuring: 'We must check on the witch!'

Hardbones and the captain hurried after Hopkins. As they ran Hardbones growled vengefully at the captain: 'If she's got away, you're going in the stocks!'

* * *

BB was sitting miserably on the straw, thinking of the fate that awaited her, when Ben appeared at the cell door.

'BB!' he called, and he produced the knife he had found and set to work trying to prise open the lock.

'Is that the best you could do?!' demanded BB, annoyed. 'Couldn't you have found a key?'

'I've opened locks with one of these before,' said Ben, and he put the point of the knife into the lock, and twisted. There was a sharp crack as the point of the blade broke off, and Ben stumbled back.

He looked despondently at the broken knife in his hand.

'Trouble is most of these locks were in wooden doors,' he said. 'I'll have to think of something else.'

BB shook her head, suddenly resigned. There was no way out, she knew it and Ben knew it.

'Ben. . . ,' she said quietly.

'What?' said Ben, studying the lock, looking for another way to open it.

'Just in case I don't get out of here, you'd better take this.'

142

Ben looked up from the lock, and found BB's hand poking through the bars holding a small key.

'That won't fit!' he said scornfully.

'It's the key to my motorbike, you idiot!' said BB. 'If you can get to it, all you have to do is put that in the slot, turn it, then when the bike starts, press the red button on the handlebars. It's pre-set to go automatically back to the twentieth century.'

Ben took the key and looked at it, dumbfounded.

'You mean, go back without you?' he said, shocked.

'You can hardly go back *with* me!' pointed out BB.

'But they're gonna burn you!' said Ben.

'I know,' said BB, and she had to turn away from him so that he wouldn't see the tears starting to well up in her eyes at the thought.

'Set fire to you! You'll burn up and . . .'

'Yes all right, there's no need to go on about it!' stormed BB, furious. 'Just get to the bike and go!'

Ben looked at the key in his hand, feeling awkward.

'I dunno what to say. . . ,' he said.

'Don't say anything,' said BB.

She reached into one of her pockets and took out a ring. She had worn it at the Chalmerstons' the previous night and had put in her pocket − nicked it, as Ben would say. She held this out to Ben through the bars of the cell door.

'Here. You should be able to sell this for quite a bit. It's an antique. Or it will be when you get back. Or maybe you might want to . . . keep it. As a memento.'

'Thanks,' said Ben, still feeling awkward about this as he pocketed the ring. He hated saying goodbye like this. He paused, then added hopefully: 'Got anything else you don't want?'

BB glared at him angrily, and he shut up, shame-faced.

'Take care of my bike,' BB said.

Then they heard the sound of footsteps approaching down the stone steps at the end of the passage and Ben dived for cover into an alcove, just as Hopkins, Hard-bones and the captain of the guard appeared, hurrying towards BB's cell.

Such was the speed at which the three men came along the passageway, and such was their intent on BB's cell, that they didn't see Ben in hiding. As soon as they had passed him Ben crept out of the alcove and then along the passage behind their backs, while Hardbones unlocked the door of BB's cell and the three men stormed in and confronted her.

'You have vanished the boy, witch!' snapped Hopkins. 'Where is he?'

BB forced a laugh.

'Oh come on! If I could do that you think I wouldn't vanish as well?'

'There is no knowing why sorcerers work the way they do.' Turning to Hardbones and the captain he muttered: 'The danger is that she has released her familiar in order that she can be released in turn. We must burn her now.'

BB stared at him, shocked.

'Now?!'

'Is the fire ready?' Hopkins demanded, looking at the captain.

'It is,' said the captain.

Desperately BB threw herself at Hopkins.

'Mr Hopkins, please. . . !' she pleaded.

Hopkins looked at her, his face stern and for-bidding.

145

'We will not give you time to practice your devilish arts on us,' he said. Then his voice softened and he added: 'Can you not see this is the only way for you to be saved?'

'Can't you see that I am not a witch!' begged BB.

Hopkins sighed and put her away from him gently into the arms of Hardbones.

'Her soul does not rest,' he said sadly. 'Take her and burn her and give her ease.'

* * *

Inside the church the door creaked open and Ben crept in, looking about him carefully. The church was empty, everyone was out looking for him.

BB's motorbike was still in the same place at the altar, and Ben crept towards it, the key in his hand.

He picked up one of the two crash helmets lying on the seat and put it on. He would do what BB had told him, he would escape back to the twentieth century. He would try and make it up to her, he would tell those other people what had happened here. Maybe they would build a statue to BB. There ought to be something to remember her by, he hoped she would like that.

He sat astride the bike, put the key in the slot and turned it. Immediately the bike started up, and Ben started to copy what he had seen BB do. Pull this lever in . . .

Suddenly the door crashed open and there in the doorway, swords drawn, stood three Roundhead soldiers.

'The boy!' cried one. 'I thought I saw him come in here!'

This was it, thought Ben. There was no going back

now. He let the clutch in and opened the throttle and the bike hurtled forward, aimed straight at the open door. The three Roundhead soldiers yelled in panic and leapt aside as Ben thundered on the bike at them.

The needle on the dial swung to the number that he remembered BB had told him. This was it. He took one hand off the handlebars and reached a finger forward to the button marked 'Time Unit.'

'Goodbye, BB!' he whispered.

Chapter Eighteen

'NO!!!' screamed BB desperately, digging her heels into the earth of the courtyard and heaving backwards, but it was no good, the captain and Hardbones jerked her sharply and she staggered forward, nearly falling, but the two men kept her moving towards the wooden stake in the middle of the yard.

Hopkins stood to one side, watching the whole process of dragging BB to the stake with an impassive expression on his face. He had seen this so often, thousands of times before. It saddened him but at the same time uplifted him: another soul saved from Satan.

Hardbones and the captain held BB against the stake, while another soldier tied a length of stout rope around her wrists and tied her to a metal ring hammered deep in the wooden post.

'I'm not a witch!' screamed BB. 'This is murder! You can't do this!!'

Other soldiers now came into the inner courtyard from the camp in the outer courtyard, and as the word spread that a witch was about to be burned even more came spilling in.

'No! Let me go!' yelled BB.

The captain picked up a length of wood which had an oil-soaked rag tied round one end. He looked at the Witchfinder General, who nodded. The captain thrust the wood into a burning brazier, and as the oil-soaked

148

rag caught light he touched it to the straw piled up around BB's feet and legs.

'NO!!!!!' screamed BB.

The straw caught light and was burning towards BB, when a sudden deep sound made everyone turn round. The next second everyone was scattering in momentary fear and panic as Ben appeared on BB's motorbike, looking as if he was having great difficulty controlling it, which he was. The bike raced through the crowd of scattering soldiers and then crashed into the burning fire, scattering burning straw around as Ben fell off the bike.

Quickly he ran to BB, pulling the broken knife from inside his coat. He slashed through the rope that tied her wrists with one swift stroke.

'Get on!' yelled Ben, pointing at the bike.

BB needed no further urging and she was running for the bike when she spotted that the HT leads from the black box Energy Amplifier at the back were still disconnected.

'You drive! I've got to fix those leads!' she yelled.

Ben jumped back astride the bike, then BB jumped on and sat backwards on the pillion, grabbing up the HT leads in both hands as Ben put the bike into gear and they shot away, heading towards the passage and the inner courtyard.

The surprised soldiers had now recovered and were pushing a cart across the passage to the outer courtyard, blocking BB's and Ben's escape.

'Shoot them!' yelled Hopkins. 'Shoot the device!'

The soldiers picked up their muskets and tried to aim at BB, Ben and the motorbike as Ben weaved the bike on an erratic pattern round and round the courtyard. BB had reconnected one of the HT leads and was desperately attempting to slot the other one in, but each time she nearly had it the bike suddenly jerked as Ben tried to dodge yet another soldier.

'Can't you ride more smoothly!' she yelled over her shoulder.

Then a volley from the soldiers' rifles rang out and they both yelled in horror as bullets smashed into the bike, and around them. BB jerked forward at this sudden shock, and the second HT lead connector slipped into the black box.

'OK! Go for it!' she yelled.

Ben opened the throttle wider and they began to speed around the inner courtyard, aiming now straight for Matthew Hopkins.

'Press the button!' yelled BB.

Matthew Hopkins's mouth opened in awe as the bike came hurtling towards him, and then Ben's finger found the 'Time Unit' button on the handlebars, pressed it, and the next second the bike folded in on itself and . . .

* * *

They were back in the tunnel of lights, going forwards, backwards, sideways, nowhere, them and the bike folding and unfolding inside outside inside outside . . .

Suddenly there was a Wooooooooswsshshshshsh-shs!!!!! then they were in a whirl of concrete and glass and there was the smell of burning rubber as the tyres hit concrete at speed. Then they bounced and were flying on the bike just off the ground, straight towards a huge glass window that reflected their image as one minute they seemed to hang suspended in mid-air while the world flashed by them. The next second there was

150

a crash of glass splintering and flying in all directions, and then they landed in the corridor of the science building with a bump that shook the breath momentarily out of both of them.

White-coated lab technicians scattered out of the bike's way as they skidded along the corridor, heading straight for the lift doors. The bike slammed into the lift, thudding against the far wall. Quickly BB flicked the button marked 'B' for basement, and the lift doors slid shut and they were going down.

* * *

BB and Ben clambered off the Yamaha and stood looking at it for a second as they got their breath back and tried to come to terms with being back in the twentieth century. The bike was pitted with the marks of bullets from the Roundheads' rifles and still had bits of straw sticking to it, some of them still scorched from the fire.

Ben was the first to speak.

'Close, eh?' he said.

Before BB could reply the door of the laboratory crashed open and Professor Crow stormed in, obviously angry. BB's and Ben's hearts sank. To go through all that, and to come back to the same problem as before.

'Dr Miller!' snapped Crow, and he stepped towards BB, and then stopped, a look of disgust on his face.

The three of them looked down, and saw that Crow had stepped in a tray of waste oil. Quickly BB looked at her Time Machine. It was intact, its chrome rods in the same condition as they had been before the explosion! Suddenly BB realized what had happened! They had arrived back in the twentieth century just a few hours *before* she had brought Ben from the past. Crow didn't yet know about Ben! He wasn't chasing after Ben at all! And if she could cover up quickly, he never would.

Crow pointed down at his oil-soaked shoe, fuming.

'What is this?' he demanded angrily.

'It's — er — it's waste oil from my motorcycle, sir,' said BB apologetically.

'This is not a garage, Dr Miller,' Crow rebuked her sternly. 'It is *supposed* to be a science laboratory.'

'Yes, sir,' said BB.

Then Crow caught sight of Ben and recoiled in surprise.

'And who on earth is *that*?'

'Er . . ,' began Ben, but BB interrupted him quickly: 'My nephew. He's . . . he's an orphan and he's come to stay with me for a while.

'Is he,' snorted Crow, not impressed. 'Well just as this place is not a garage, neither is it a home for your unfortunate relatives.'

'No, sir,' said BB, hoping to keep the conversation short.

'Good,' said Crow crisply. 'I am here because I understand that you made a most unusual entry into this building just now, Dr Miller. Through a window.'

'Er . . . yes. I'm afraid I lost control of the bike.'

'Do you realize how much damage you have done?' Crow demanded.

'I'll pay for it,' said BB. 'Every penny. I'm truly sorry and it won't happen again.'

'No it certainly won't!' snapped Crow, determined to drive the point home.

'No, it won't,' agreed BB, the expression on her face showing that she was truly sorry.

Crow looked at her, puzzled. This wasn't like

Miller at all. Where was the defiance in her eyes, the snappy comeback?

'Aren't you about to come up with some witty answer, Dr Miller?' he said, sniffily.

'No, sir. You are quite right in all you say, Sir,' affirmed BB.

'Yes, I am,' said Crow.

'Yes, you certainly are,' said BB again, nodding to emphasize this fact.

Crow frowned. This definitely wasn't like Miller. There was something wrong here, but he just couldn't put his finger on it.

'You're not ill, are you?' asked Crow, becoming worried. The last thing they wanted was an infection of some kind in the science building.

BB shook her head.

'No, I'm fine,' she said.

'Then it must be shock,' said Crow.

And with that he turned and headed towards the door. BB and Ben heaved sighs of relief, which stopped in mid-sigh as Crow stopped and pointed at BB's time machine.

'As for that so-called "Time Machine" of yours, it'll never work,' he said in a superior tone.

BB allowed herself a little secret smile.

'You never know, Professor Crow,' she said in as airy a manner as she could manage. 'We'll keep trying.'

They watched Crow as he continued towards the door. At the door he stopped and looked at BB and Ben. He still had this lingering feeling that something wasn't right, but he just couldn't put his finger on it. He shrugged. He would find out. After all, he was head of the science faculty, secrets didn't remain secret from him for long.

As the door shut behind Crow, BB and Ben looked at each other, delight on their faces. They had done it! They were safe! And so was the Time Machine!

Delightedly BB patted the seat of her now even more precious Yamaha.

'OK, kid,' she said. 'Where do you fancy going?'

Other great reads ⟨ *from* **Red Fox**

Further Red Fox titles that you might enjoy reading are listed on the following pages. They are available in bookshops or they can be ordered directly from us.

   If you would like to order books, please send this form and the money due to:

ARROW BOOKS, BOOKSERVICE BY POST, PO BOX 29, DOUGLAS, ISLE OF MAN, BRITISH ISLES. Please enclose a cheque or postal order made out to Arrow Books Ltd for the amount due, plus 22p per book for postage and packing, both for orders within the UK and for overseas orders.

NAME _____

ADDRESS _____

_____

Please print clearly.

Whilst every effort is made to keep prices low, it is sometimes necessary to increase cover prices at short notice. If you are ordering books by post, to save delay it is advisable to phone to confirm the correct price. The number to ring is THE SALES DEPARTMENT 071 (if outside London) 973 9700.

Other great reads **from Red Fox**

THE SNIFF STORIES Ian Whybrow

Things just keep happening to Ben Moore. It's dead hard avoiding disaster when you've got to keep your street cred with your mates *and* cope with a family of oddballs at the same time. There's his appalling 2½ year old sister, his scatty parents who are into healthy eating and animal rights and, worse than all of these, there's Sniff! If only Ben could just get on with his scientific experiments and his attempt at a world beating *Swampbeast* score . . . but there's no chance of that while chaos is just around the corner.

ISBN 0 09 9750406   £2.50

J.B. SUPERSLEUTH Joan Davenport

James Bond is a small thirteen-year-old with spots and spectacles. But with a name like that, how can he help being a supersleuth?

It all started when James and 'Polly' (Paul) Perkins spotted a teacher's stolen car. After that, more and more mysteries needed solving. With the case of the Arabian prince, the Murdered Model, the Bonfire Night Murder and the Lost Umbrella, JB's reputation at Moorside Comprehensive soars.

But some of the cases aren't quite what they seem . . .

ISBN 0 09 9717808   £1.99

Other great reads ⟍ *from* **Red Fox**

The Maggie Series   Joan Lingard

MAGGIE 1: THE CLEARANCE

Sixteen-year-old Maggie McKinley's dreading the prospect of a whole summer with her granny in a remote Scottish glen. But the holiday begins to look more exciting when Maggie meets the Frasers. She soon becomes best friends with James and spends almost all her time with him. Which leads, indirectly, to a terrible accident . . .

ISBN 0 09 947730 0   £1.99

MAGGIE 2: THE RESETTLING

Maggie McKinley's family has been forced to move to a high rise flat and her mother is on the verge of a nervous breakdown. As her family begins to rely more heavily on her, Maggie finds less and less time for her schoolwork and her boyfriend James. The pressures mount and Maggie slowly realizes that she alone must control the direction of her life.

ISBN 0 09 949220 2   £1.99

MAGGIE 3: THE PILGRIMAGE

Maggie is now seventeen. Though a Glaswegian through and through, she is very much looking forward to a cycling holiday with her boyfriend James. But James begins to annoy Maggie and tensions mount. Then they meet two Canadian boys and Maggie finds she is strongly attracted to one of them.

ISBN 0 09 951190 8   £2.50

MAGGIE 4: THE REUNION

At eighteen, Maggie McKinley has been accepted for university and is preparing to face the world. On her first trip abroad, she flies to Canada to a summer au pair job and a reunion with Phil, the Canadian student she met the previous summer. But as usual in Maggie's life, events don't go quite as planned . . .

ISBN 0 09 951260 2   £2.50

Other great reads *from* **Red Fox**

Discover the great animal stories of Colin Dann

JUST NUFFIN

The Summer holidays loomed ahead with nothing to look forward to except one dreary week in a caravan with only Mum and Dad for company. Roger was sure he'd be bored.

But then Dad finds Nuffin: an abandoned puppy who's more a bundle of skin and bones than a dog. Roger's holiday is transformed and he and Nuffin are inseparable. But Dad is adamant that Nuffin must find a new home. Is there *any* way Roger can persuade him to change his mind?

ISBN 0 09 966900 5   £1.99

KING OF THE VAGABONDS

'You're very young,' Sammy's mother said, 'so heed my advice. Don't go into Quartermile Field.'

His mother and sister are happily domesticated but Sammy, the tabby cat, feels different. They are content with their lot, never wondering what lies beyond their immediate surroundings. But Sammy is burningly curious and his life seems full of mysteries. Who is his father? Where has he gone? And what is the mystery of Quartermile Field?

ISBN 0 09 957190 0   £2.50

Other great reads ✎ *from* **Red Fox**

**Haunting fiction for older readers from
Red Fox**

THE XANADU MANUSCRIPT
John Rowe Townsend

There is nothing unusual about visitors in Cambridge.

So what is it about three tall strangers which fills John with a mixture of curiosity and unease? Not only are they strikingly handsome but, for apparently educated people, they are oddly surprised and excited by normal, everyday events. And, as John pursues them, their mystery only seems to deepen.

Set against a background of an old university town, this powerfully compelling story is both utterly fantastic and oddly convincing.

'An author from whom much is expected and received.'
Economist

ISBN 0 09 9751801   £2.50

ONLOOKER   Roger Davenport

Peter has always enjoyed being in Culver Wood, and dismissed the tales of hauntings, witchcraft and superstitions associated with it. But when he starts having extraordinary visions that are somehow connected with the wood, and which become more real to him than his everyday life, he realizes that something is taking control of his mind in an inexplicable and frightening way.

Through his uneasy relationship with Isobel and her father, a Professor of Archaeology interested in excavating Culver Wood, Peter is led to the discovery of the wood's secret and his own terrifying part in it.

ISBN 0 09 9750708   £2.50